MY BEAUTIFUL CITY AUSTIN

MY BEAUTIFUL CITY AUSTIN

David Heymann

JOHN HARDY PUBLISHING

HOUSTON, TEXAS

MY BEAUTIFUL CITY AUSTIN

FIRST EDITION
FIRST PRINT 2014

10 9 8 7 6 5 4 3 2 1

ISBN: 978-0-9903714-0-3

Cover Design by David Heymann

Printed in Canada
Printed at Friesens Corporation

John Hardy Publishing
Houston, Texas

for Sandy

MY BEAUTIFUL CITY AUSTIN

A Wish from Without

Intern Owners

The Honey Trap

A Life in Ruins

Patterns of Passive Aggression

Keeping Austin Weird

Gatherings on the Line

A Wish from Without

A Wish from Without

Regardless of the direction from which you arrive — except, obviously, coming south on the Interstate — you will, rising over some ridge or passing beyond the eye shadow of a range of hills, suddenly see the whole city of Austin as if in a bowl set before you. Coming over the Onion Creek ridge at dusk, or dropping out of the western hills on Redbud Trail, or climbing the freeway overpass as the MoPac hits 71 and 290, or just between the hills with the big blinking antennas along the 360 Loop, or turning in to — really looping up onto — the parking lot at the Travis County Exposition Center, it's just a freakish thing about how the city sits in the landscape, and the distance at which you invariably see it. The whole of it appears below the horizon, and so it feels discrete and knowable and oddly comforting.

It was true, until recently, that, during the half hour prior to your seeing Austin in this extraordinary way, you would have been traveling through nothing very much resembling the scar tissue of a city, so the view afforded itself to your eyes for a few seconds before your mind came into focus. It wasn't like coming out of the tunnel and *WHAM*: Pittsburgh! You were always far enough away, and it seemed you had enough time (though it couldn't have been more than seven or eight seconds at speed), that you could perceive the whole of the not-so-large central city — it rises in light from a continuous scruff-hazy brown-greenness — and recognize the consequences of its singular order: the biggish buildings rising along Congress Avenue to the dome of the capitol on the first great hill up from the river, the library tower marking the university on the next great hill north, the varied higher ground, and high hills to the west. You couldn't see the Colorado River, which, with Waller and Shoal Creeks, brackets the whole, but you could sense it in the way the city is tightened. If you drove in at dusk or dawn you could still see the remnant plane of moonlight towers.

But, still true today, you only get that panoptic view once on any trip, and, more powerfully still, all of the points from which the view is afforded, gates though they may be, do not yet mark entry into the city. You drop back down into a disquieting dry grass and stunted oak-motte rural — it seems abandoned — and Austin disappears entirely. It's as if the city as a discrete and powerful whole had welled up from the bottom of some still stream or lake and roiled the surface before vanishing, leaving in its wake only an image of desire. The earliest memory I have of Austin

is, as a ten-year-old, being awakened by the collective
sighing appreciation of passengers on a bus as the city
so sparkled into view just at sunset. The bus drove on
into darkness, and we did not stop.

Indeed it is some miles before any sort of city
seems to begin again, and by then you are quite close
in. You could easily be fooled by that. Once, driving
through from Houston in early summer after the
11th grade, I stopped with some friends up on Mount
Bonnell. It was the border of what seemed city at that
time, although it's no more than a few miles north-
west of downtown. We sat looking west over the
southward tending thinness of Lake Austin, one of
a series of poseur lakes that serve to emasculate the
Colorado as it comes carving out of the hills onto the
flat farmed plains to the east. The high hills west, for
as far as the eye could see, were carpeted with ashe
juniper — which people here call *cedar* — hairy, itchy
trees. Someone lit a joint: we smoked and looked some
more. In the patches between the trees you could see
bare limestone ground, and a visceral heat seemed to
curtain up. Black and turkey vultures floated on the
heat, and all in all it seemed clear that over there was
a pretty marvelous place not to be. And in my mind
that hardness, with the river between, added to the
allure of the city.

Late the same day we headed west across the Colorado just below where that lake — Lake Austin — ends at the Tom Miller Dam just above Red Bud Isle. We drove up into the scruffy, dusty forest, expecting to find it barren. But — and here is where the part about it fooling you comes around — it wasn't that way. For one thing, there were a lot of little houses strewn about amid the trees: mostly fieldstone, lap siding, screen porch, gravel drive, carport. From above they had been invisible because the cedar make a tight canopy about a story and a half high, and the houses were all under the canopy. Even underneath you could only half see them through the many trunks and the filtered patchy light, the high grass and the rolling topography, and the fact that the houses didn't seem to attend to the road. You could glimpse bits and signs of a sort of happy, cockaigne-eater inhabitation: a shirt still draped over a folding lawn chair, stacked lumber gone gray, a pool float propped against an open car door, the cab light off or out, though little of it felt derelict.

By now we had made a right turn from the road climbing up from the dam and were driving north. The new road was running parallel to the lake, more or less along a continuous contour, making alternating convex and concave curves as it rounded the shoulders of the hills, then crossed the drainages — or washes, as they are more aptly called. A few miles along, the road abruptly gut-dipped to cross a small, dark creek, and as it did so a view down to the lake synchronously opened and closed to our right. It was like watching through the shutter of an old camera during a slow, maybe one-second exposure: *bizzzzzzzzup*. Everyone in the car swiveled hard right, and, interested and immediately in agreement, we slowed to a stop, then slowly rolled backward and angled off along the road about thirty yards above the dip, where other cars were also pulled over, and got out.

The swale below the road's shoulder running down to the dip was filled with flowering purple thistle, which continued partway up the far bank. It was quite warm on the road, the sun slanting over the hills, and with the engine off there was buzzing all around. Little black-and-yellow birds — lesser goldfinch — flitted between the thistle and the scrub cedar beyond, making sad two-note whistles. At the dip there was a gap in the thistle, and passing through the gap you had to jump down over limestone ledges to enter the sharp valley, dark with large live oak trees spreading over the creek, telescoping to the bright lake. Just under the outer edges of the oaks' horizontal spread, on the upslope side, there were more shack houses, and along the creek there were a few docks, just wood piers stuck pleasantly straight out over the water. At the road clear water flowed in the bed (there were tiny fossil oysters exposed), but ahead the water of the creek was still and broadening. Really, it was just the constant waterline of the green lake.

Out at the point where the creek valley rounded into the lake you could see some people out in the water — mostly adults? — sort of swim-lolling. There were a number of inflatable rafts, and no one seemed to be moving, like a herd of manatees. Every now and then a motorboat would pass the opening of the creek, and the valley would fill with noise, then drain. A hundred yards in we came upon a limestone ledge where people had left clothes and belongings, and set coolers and stacked small pyramids of empty beer cans. The nature of the place — was it private property? — was confounding. There was little evidence of public accountability, nor deterrent to trespass beyond the occasional rotting edge of a cedar fence, or just prickly pear hedge.

We took off our shoes and waded into the lake, in shorts. It was glorious. Getting wet is always better than you expect: you arrive. The water from without had seemed murky, but when in it, it was clear and cooling, the silty greenness coming from somewhere below. Swimming out from the creek we passed groups of swim-floaters, but no one seemed to question our presence, at least as much as that could be determined by how anyone looked at or spoke to us: *hey man; hey.*

There was an invisible boundary where the creek ended and the lake began. It was just a point where you stopped relaxing and began thinking about the motorboats. Underwater you could hear the high-pitched whine of their propellers, even at a great distance. I would swim a few strokes, then abruptly stop to tread water. The other swimmers were on the creek side of the line, and gradually I treaded my way back there too. But I was still far enough out in the lake that, even at water level, I could, looking back toward the hills, see the extent of the live oaks along the valley and make out the little houses under the foliage.

The oaks were startlingly large. Their size had been perfectly hidden by the dropping valley floor, so that the top of their canopy matched in elevation the cedar to either side. You know all of that emptiness around the city? That was just a *WISH*. But it was also called Austin. We swam in and pulled our shoes on and, no one saying very much to avoid spoiling the pleasure of having successfully interloped, we began our walk under the live oaks back to the car.

Live oak leaves are dark green above. As the tree grows the inner branches die, so the leaf cover moves out slowly, like the expanding sphere of a dying star. Ball moss colonizes the dying branches. The undersides of the leaves are silver-gray, and the shade is at once dense, open, and radiant. But not much grows in it. The trail — it was just the soil compacted — crossed along over the open ground moving from shade shell to shade shell along the water. This I remember as clearly now as then. Just as we came out into the sun from under one great tree there appeared, coming toward us from the next, a woman — in her early twenties? — brown hair, the same color as her tan skin and parted in the center, beautiful, and naked, save for a pair of white flip-flops and a wash-thinned cotton towel trailing down to her ankles from a rolling around her waist. Printed on the towel was a picture of Yosemite Sam in highest dudgeon, with that gleeful angry maniacal rat terrier leer, and guns already out but pointed down, his equally pointed elbows up: *Aaaaaaaaahm A Comin Fer Ya!* As she walked toward us without any seeming modesty or awareness thereof, Sam — life-size, upright, front-facing

— seemed to be walking just ahead of her, her larger steps giving his stride the perfect stalking amplitude as he came across the clearing.

Yosemite Sam, exposed breasts, that dreamy telescoping creek: heroes all. To be precise, that's the kind of information teenage boys do not have the capacity to process. As with any other near-death experience you pretend to be as cool as possible, then a little later you stagger around. The reverse is also true. You can be staggering around for a while before you can admit that events of the utmost seriousness have transpired. In 1996 I moved to Austin in hope — I'll get to the details — and the first thing I did when I got into town was go back up to Mount Bonnell. I parked the car in the lot along the roadcut below and to the east of the summit, and climbed the stone stairs to the flat top of the mountain.

That stairway is an almost entirely continuous hundred and some steep steps, like a stalled escalator moving up through the scrub. Its upper lip coincides with the start of a sort of bald spot on top, though you can't see much just as you come out at that point. In front of you, along the western edge of the bald spot, is a pergola that angles back and forth along the top of the cliff. Tourists, the retired, couples and young families, old hippies, UT students, and the generally horny flock to the top of Mount Bonnell and colonize the low wall under the pergola to watch the sun go down. But they have pretty wildly varying needs. The wall can serve as a photographic backdrop, a safety barrier, or a playground, but sometimes it's a privacy shield for heavy petting. So you approach it with some trepidation, half-waiting to see what pops up. And since the ground is still rising slightly — and you have to step around some mediocre historical shrap — it isn't until you're just upon it that the view of the western hills opens before and below you.

Oh man! There were kids in high school who would suddenly, from one day to the next, be assaulted by a kind of virulent, weeping, unrestrainable acne. Where before there had been a hot hairy emptiness, now as far west as you could see these steroidal houses, huge and tall and gross and unseemly and pretentious, were erupting out of the cedar forest like a horrid skin condition, an outburst of limestone whiteheads. The hills on the northern horizon were carpeted with a vast eczema of limestone slathered starter mansions, cheek by jowl, spreading southward unchecked. Below me in the lake an immense long landfill had materialized — is that allowed? — replete with the most unseemly disproportionate private construc-

tions: eight thousand? ten thousand? square foot....
houses? — all severed behind a tall steel and limestone wall that you could see crashing through the
underbrush like the International Date Line. Everywhere you could make out piles of orange lumber
and roof tiles — everywhere you could see the white
pickup trucks of contractors and builders. From the
myriad construction sites a powdery white limestone
dust rose up in a ringing haze, coating the trees.

You probably remember in *Star Wars* when Luke
returns in his hover car to find — unimaginable night-
mare — the smoldering remnants of his family home.
It was like that, only backward. Now the Empire had
struck back by *building* the house, the overripe family
dream house, and all of Luke's kin — everyone in fact
— was in the grip of a darkly forceful materialistic
nostalgia. I know you know the house, because some
version of it is the same everywhere in America. The
idea is to take any prewar house type and inflate it to
fit all the new crap that has to go inside it, in support
of the new interiority. But even then it's not enough,
and often the old models are compounds, like farms or
villas. So Luke pulls his Range Rover into what appears
to be the stables, but it's really the three-car garage,
sculpted rafter tails under the eaves, gray stained
cypress against stone, all asymmetrical memories.

The sun was going down, but it seemed lighter and hotter. I stepped back from the edge, overwhelmed by a sucking hollowness. Surrounded by everyone's pleasure — the hills and houses, the river and the mountain, the tourists along the wall — I could not see myself in anything. Until just that moment Austin had naively existed in my mind as an antidote to the overstuffed burrito-ness of America. But what struck me then was that all of the reasons I wanted to move to Austin were the same as everyone else's reasons. I felt sick, and was flooded with a sense of having made a deep mistake, of being too late. I turned around and walked back down to my car, and sat in the front seat, sweating in doubt.

But, you know, as I sat there, I fought it off. I really wanted to stay in my beautiful city, and I decided that it had to be OK. I thought about it hard then, and I've thought about it a lot since. I wish I could say my reasons were noble, but they weren't — they aren't. When you start in architecture, especially when you first start studying architecture, it's all high-mindedness, a hangover from the Frank Lloyd Wright *Fountainhead* idea of architects actually having a say in the way the world becomes. But Wright could behave the way he did, telling people how to live, because he had work, and everything in architecture, all authority and identity, stems from having work. When I got out of school in the late eighties there wasn't any work, and it wasn't clear that work would come. It was a long, hungry stretch.

That didn't stop architects from talking about how the world should be. Quite the contrary: it was a feverish time for arguing about how architecture would be the antidote, and during those years a lot of architects made careers just from ideas. Working in architecture is correctly called *practice*, and that's how it felt, like practice for something important coming in the future. Still, it was grim, all skimmings and parings, nothing to make a dent in the substantial. You had to do ridiculous work: the first task I had at my first job in an architect's office was cleaning pigeon shit off the skylight over the studio.

Then — it seemed like overnight as the nineties began — there was way too much work. Everyone, all the recession survivors, had work, and obscene budgets. Here is the weird thing. All the thinking and arguing that had gone on, the more finely knowing how the world should be made, that all vanished. A strange generational wariness set in, about covering your ass. And that became institutionalized in the recent downturn, which Austin, at least for architects

making high-end houses, barely registered. It became
— it remains — bad form to complain about or con-
front the odd cosmological desires of your clients, the
peculiar nature of their projects, or what is happen-
ing to the landscape, because underneath everything
there is only the shame of the memory of no jobs. It's
bad form to *disagree*. That's me, to be sure. I climbed
back up the stairs to the top of Mount Bonnell. And
before and below me, looking down, was the incon-
trovertible evidence that, sickening or not, there was,
at least, work to be had here as an architect.

I decided that my disappointment was the first
sign of becoming old badly, like complaining about
computers or cell phones. I mean, landscapes change,
and their paths ignore whiners. The more I stood
there thinking, the more I convinced myself of the
essential impossibility of pinpointing the exact ethical
dimension. People do not, I told myself, build with
maliced intent. They build to be happy, and it was
only my problem that I didn't get their happiness.
I looked out over that brightening vast emptiness,
steadied myself, and saw my busy future.

Intern Owners

Intern Owners

So I started making houses for the newly wealthy. It would, on the surface, seem hard to make something for someone just learning to own — an intern owner — and having to learn to own a house and a killer chunk of land in the same pass. House-building costs a lot, property costs a lot. No two ways about it: to amass that kind of cash you typically have to be an asshole, or be genetically related to one, and in the path of their cash flow. Then the money floods in and shapes up the high ground, and sanctifies that whole way of being, to people, to things and buildings, and to pieces of the world, and other possessions. Or, it can be more complicated than that: you can really work for it. Doctors and lawyers do that. But with them there is always the dark question of motive: cash or service? A lot of the ones I know can't resolve that question for themselves either, but who says it needs to be resolved?

The first house I worked on — it was my ride back to Texas — was for my older cousin Kyle Eubanks and his wife Janice, and their family. Kyle was a dermatologist, specializing in the removal of skin cancers, but his genius was as a medical businessman. He had capitalized on the Preferred Provider shift with independent clinics to meet the demand of a malignant sky. "We'd do it drive-through if the AMA would let us." I understood the profit base, having burned my entire youth. I'd already had a problematic mole excised in New York. It was black with a profile like a dead squirrel. The doctor was sweet enough not to mention its obvious cancerousness until the biopsy came back. The mole was just below my right nipple, and she first removed it with a round metal punch, like taking a tiny core sample. Later, when I went back in, the doctor cut out a circular indentation about an inch and a quarter in diameter, and maybe an eighth of an inch deep. For some seconds fluid oozed into the little crater. The doctor sewed the edges together in a straight line across the center. It looked like an eye on a shrunken head.

There wasn't really anything unusual about the house that Kyle and Janice wanted. Mostly, they wanted it to look like some mythical older houses in the Hill Country: a simple limestone structure, with proper rooms, porches, a pitched metal roof — something that connected them with the built heritage of the landscape. That is what almost everyone wants here. The word Kyle and Janice used was *unpretentious*. I think every client I've ever had has said that at some point, though it's an odd enough word, when you think about it. I mean, the houses being refer-enced were dirt-poor shacks — *less than the trees* — in no way able to accommodate the scale of people's lives nowadays. And also, because this part of the country is growing fast, almost no one who wants a house like that actually grew up here, so there's an underlying level of pretense at work no matter how you cut it. Not that there is a problem with architec-tures of pretense; there's a whole history of that. Still, there is this central mystery for me, about the *oppor-tunity* here, to *not* build that way, which arises solely from the circumstances of this place, the landscape, and the way of life, all of which Austin is famous for, but which is undercut every time a new house is built in the dream of the Hill Country, like killing an elephant with cotton balls.

I'd known Kyle in spurts growing up in Hous-ton. His dad — my uncle, an old-school academic moralist — taught in the biology department at Rice. Kyle was a couple of years older than me. He would occasionally host late-night stoner parties atop the biology building. The scientists stored oblong and conic rubber flask stoppers in big crates up there. These, when hurled at the concrete walks below, would bounce off at highly unpredictable angles. Kyle had an attractive, provoking honesty, and a series of terrific girlfriends. Each of these relationships lasted surprisingly long, but — perhaps because he seemed to resist any kind of seriousness as a matter of principle — he'd always be left behind, usually for someone with a mystical edge, or just someone more vague. I think he privately took these breakups seriously, and he matured secretly in the dark intervals. Maybe there weren't enough intervals, or the onset of middle age erased their consequence. Whenever we met to discuss the house without Janice, he would insist on taking me to a *Hooters*. There was one near the site of the old Armadillo World Headquarters, the epicenter of the Austin music scene before it was bulldozed for a state government building.

Kyle was already effortlessly intelligent as a kid, and smart enough to not care about showing it. He was accepted to MIT, but chose to come to UT. I remember he *disappeared* into Austin. I visited him here once on spring break when I was a freshman in college in New York City. He'd been in Austin for several years, really stretching out his degree plan, and was living with various roommates in this two-story wooden house on the bluff above Pease Park, which runs along Shoal Creek, the original western edge of the city. Upstairs the house had four small, reflectively symmetrical bedrooms under the sloping eaves. It was unclear that anyone claimed any of the rooms, given the desultory evidence. There might be just a mattress, some milk crates of clothes, a Luxo lamp, whatever, the walls bare.

The bedrooms flanked a stair hall and a broad, deep balcony that was embedded in the back of the house. It projected out like a Polaroid toward the trees along the creek. The sloping roof slid past the balcony about midway out. Beyond that the rail had been removed. I arrived in the late afternoon to find seven or eight people, shoeless and variously undressed for the warmth, laid out there side by side on their stomachs — brown beer bottles here and there — with their heads at the far end, all staring intently out at the trees. I said *hello*, to no particular acknowledgment. Kyle looked back over his shoulder, and smiling — *hey* — slowly got up on his knees, waved me down, whispering, "here, take my slot," and vanished into the house. I lay down, and looked out into the trees: they were fairly nice red oaks and cedar elms. Taking my cue from the others, I stared at them as hard as I could. But I didn't get it. There was a girl just to my right, and after a few minutes I turned to her — she had her chin on her hands, which glowed a deep bright orange — "Listen, what is it?"

"What is what?"

"What is it that everyone is looking at?"

"Oh" — slowly opening her eyes quite wide — "the owls, of course."

"Owls?"

She looked to the red oak, then back at me: "Kyle calls them Shadrach, Meshach, and Abednego."

I looked again, focusing at different depths through the trees. Then, all at once, resolving themselves as whole objects, I saw three young owls — they were almost the size of turkeys, but perfectly hidden by color and pattern — sitting in full view, dead level forty feet away on the near limb of a big red oak: young great horned owls. The owls stared back, neither moving nor blinking their yellow eyes. It was really shocking to me that I had completely missed them. I was in equal parts amazed and embarrassed.

After some moments I turned to my neighbor again: "What do *you* call them?"

"I call them Snap, Crackle, and Pop."

"In honor of the breakfast cereal?"

"In honor of their relationship with squirrels."

I turned to look at the owls some more. Their flight feathers were showing through down. I looked over the lip of the porch: the base of the tree was studded with their regurgitated pellets. Gradually dusk came on. Suddenly — silently — the owls flew off, and the trance-like state on the porch broke up in laughter. Downstairs, Kyle had been making food with other friends that had arrived: salad, guacamole, warm tortillas, more beer. There were three big picnic tables set end to end to form a very long table that started in the nominal dining room but continued into a larger living room through an archway, the table so tight against one side of the rounded opening that the fixed bench of the table there had been cut away.

All the windows were open. The conversation just roamed and bubbled along, almost entirely about people and situations particular to the city and the university. If it was hard to break in or take part, I didn't feel uncomfortable. No one seemed to be put either on or off by my presence, new to me. The conversation just stayed in the present tense. I asked the girl I had been next to on the porch — Linda, apparently Kyle's girlfriend — about her orange hands: "I eat a bag of carrots every day." No further explanation was forthcoming, nor seemed warranted. Later we all went dancing at a bar downtown, and it stayed much the same way. No one partnered up exclusively, so the dancing wasn't especially seductive or sexual. It was just a continuous euphoria that, real or imagined, was never called into question by anyone's overt agenda. Very late we climbed over the fence to skinny-dip at Barton Springs. Somehow all of these people were getting degrees from the University of Texas.

By way of contrast, at the time I was living in Brooklyn, where it was still miserable mid-winter, in a loft conversion that only had commercial heat, which is during working hours, while you were away at your job or school. Steam rose when you peed in the toilet in the morning, then it was cold again when you came home. I was living under a sort of cloud, thinking I needed to *like* New York. But I could never get used to the sense that people there measured the entirely arbitrary circumstances that controlled your life as an accurate indicator of your abilities. Like, someone would happen down a street just as the perfect chair was being pitched out, and that was an indication of talent. In every conversation it seemed you were being bludgeoned with peoples' competitive chance histories. Everyone treated New York, the city itself, religiously, as if it were ultimately judging them. So I was really taken by the conversation in Austin. People didn't seem to need to convince you with their *project*; no positioning seemed to be taking place. By contrast, in New York it was everyone else's own agenda, always.

To make matters worse, I was sharing my apartment with two other architecture students, a couple, romantically involved. Among their many upsetting pathological habits, they bought all of their books (two of each) by *size*. It is probably less impressive that they did so — "We really need some more ten-inch books" — than that they could so guilelessly and cheerfully admit to it. Those two are now successful academics. There should of course be a biblical injunction against the coupling of architects. Architects are wired to relate by denial. It's their own brand of competitive snobbery. If there is any erotic attraction, the repression builds to a fever pitch and both parties implode. It's painful to witness — it is almost as bad with classical musicians — and taxing and distasteful to imagine into the future. People regularly comment on the organized nature of architects' houses, but there's a difference between order and orderliness. Think of the children, cleaning their preordained rooms, continually forced to recognize their parents' more abiding love for the arguable design intentions of, for example, some great, dead Scandinavian. A wretched youth!

Kyle married Janice in 1985 — she was already seven months pregnant with Emily. The wedding was held in a field out above Hamilton Pool, in the early summer. The Unitarian minister, the groom — both in linen shorts and Mexican wedding shirts — and all the guests had gathered under one large live oak, waiting for the remainder of the wedding party, which proceeded out from another great oak, across a flowering field, to join the ceremony. The procession was led by two young girls smothered in more flowers, and these two, rather than marching straight and true to their destination, kept meandering around fire ant mounds invisible to those not crossing through the shin-high grass. The bride (in a pale yellow silk sundress) and her friends were laughing as they followed, but her father was slightly red-faced. That was the whole tone of the day: the people from Austin, and the people from anywhere else.

After the ceremony, the wedding party spent the afternoon down in the glorious caldera, floating in inner tubes near the waterfall. Hamilton Pool sits west of Austin, now in the city's path, but then in the relative isolation of the dryer upland over the Pedernales River valley, near Bee Caves. The stream there, cutting through a layer of harder limestone above, carved out a circular cavern in the softer limestone below, that, collapsing in on itself, formed a sinkhole almost entirely surrounded by the overhanging cliff, which cantilevers in a perfect arc well out over the water. The stream waterfalls in from above, and there is a thin beachlet just at the point that the large pool drains further into a stream running down to the Pedernales. From above, all of it is invisible, and coming upon the grotto from the path that wends down into the valley, then backtracks up into the caldera, is like being let in on an important secret.

Someone had wrapped two inner tubes together with white fabric, like the sign for infinity, for Kyle and Janice, and surrounded these with other inner tubes. Sporadically people would swim or float out refreshments from the beach to join the raft. I ended up in a tube next to Janice and her glorious belly. She was from Houston too, which surprised me, since the wedding was in Austin. Houston is a strange city in which to grow up. No one *should* live there. The relentless torpor — the heat, the humidity — starts rotting everything before it's even finished being built. No one expects anything to last — I think even pets die prematurely — so there is no real sense of a lost past. The city is constantly metastasizing unchecked and un-zoned. For years the only limit was something like you couldn't open a porno shop within 500 feet of a school or church. That said, it's still dull. When you talk to people in Houston, the conversation is always about waiting for their lives to *happen*. So instead we talked about our mutual desire to live in Austin. Janice said: "What I like here is you can do what you want." On the surface that made sense, but later on it struck me as wrong. Houston was where you could do what you wanted.

Midway through the conversation Janice startled me: "So, David … will you design a house for us?" Just as she said it, Kyle tilted his head back — "It has to be the perfect Austin house" — then he was back in another conversation. Another tube of champagne had just arrived, and I wasn't taking any of it seriously, given the mild goofiness of the whole event, beyond, of course, saying that I would absolutely do it. Kyle was just finishing his medical internship in San Antonio, where he'd met Janice, who was a nurse. But they were already planning their move back to Austin. Of his group of friends, he was the first to consciously start a future *track*. Moving from tube to tube, I talked to some of his Austin friends, and I kept hearing that, for each person, a little panic had set in. This always came out as a mild disbelief in Kyle's decision to go to med school, and to get married to Janice, who wasn't really known to anyone, and whose very apparent pregnancy in a swimsuit, connected as it were with Kyle formalizing his life, seemed to signal the end of something. I think this might have been true anywhere, but it seemed there was a peculiar underlying hope that was distinct, that the whole point of living in Austin was never having to take any of these kinds of terrifying steps.

I thought about it on the flight back to New York, and held it up in hope at random intervals. There really wasn't a place I knew in the world for which I would rather design a house. It was partly the landscape, but mostly it was the way of life, and how living in the landscape was an extension of the whole way of being that seemed to have developed there. You could easily imagine it — simple transitions between outside and in, many kinds of shade, the rooms smaller than needed, because you could use the outside to make them feel larger, everything modest, except for ridiculous sliding glass doors everywhere, a house you wouldn't necessarily look at, but a setting for a life lived easily between a fireplace and a carport, and the life itself without formal constraint, or simple definitions, an ongoing experiment, so you could make a house out to the drip lines of the trees where you never had to wear shoes, and a bed or table would just roll outside, and you could find a place in the sun or the breeze or both or not. This is harder to say, but the house I had in mind was sort of against everything that I hated about architecture too, about making the airless perfect artifact in the uninhabited photograph. In my mind I had an idea about a house that only made sense if there were people living in it.

So, right at the start of 1996, they called to see if I would consider designing their house. I was still in New York, interning on forgettable buildings for mediocre architects. You legally intern before passing the licensing exam, usually three years after your degree. Supposedly you solidify your professional mastery under the tutelage of a responsible practitioner. But the practitioner is always too busy to help, and you learn that there is way too much to learn. You learn, instead, to fake it — to owners, contractors, subs, engineers, officials, building committees, neighborhood groups, acquaintances, friends, family: everyone. It exacts a hellish toll on your psyche. You know they know.

Little changes when you pass the licensing exam. The real difference between an intern and an architect is that the architect gets the work, and the responsibility, and the credit, even if not doing the actual labor. You can't evolve from one to the other. Working for someone else — you could be licensed or not, and you could literally be the only person who knows anything about the actual building — you still feel there's a two-by-four lodged between the left and right lobes of your brain.

So, after the horrid realization creeps over you that getting the work is the issue, there follows an awakening about what it might take to get work: genetics, fawning slime, client theft. Increasingly you see your future as if through binoculars set backward: small and repulsively distant. Few succeed — it's always the least deserving — and they all tell a story of being miraculously commissioned, as if in a dream, no strings, no limit, no having to explain the things architects like but no one else understands, like continuous flush reveals. Anyone should be able to pull it off. But really they mean: you will never, ever, break out. As, one by one, your contemporaries are lifted from your lingering purgatory, or fall out the bottom, you become desperate enough to leap with the flimsiest prospect — a renovation, a kitchen, something for your parents, maybe even teaching. When the phone rang I was sitting at my drafting station with my head down, having just left a partner's windowed office. I had been given the honor to redesign a hospital wing to reduce its budget by the exact amount it had cost the client to hire a consultant to examine the cost. I decided to move to Austin instead.

Kyle and Janice were living in a small two-bedroom house built in the thirties in Travis Heights, an older neighborhood that rises up along Blunn Creek just south of the river downtown. Their house was near the warm springs pool at the upper end of the park that follows the creek. Everything about the way they seemed in the house was easy and loose. In the kitchen the breakfast table was completely covered with stickers the kids had peeled off of years worth of bananas. Janice had shellacked them into perpetuity. They had built a shower in the backyard. Its edge was part of a woven wood-slat back fence, so the neighbor's dog would peer up at you through the gaps. Kyle liked to take people out in the backyard at night to see the stars through the city sky using night-vision binoculars — that works startlingly well. They'd had a second daughter, Maya, and Emily was on the verge of middle school. The girls had been sharing one small room and so their life flowed all over the house. This was one of the big reasons they were moving. Maya was going to start at an Episcopal school in the western hills, and they wanted to be closer.

And then Kyle and Janice were getting older too and they wanted something more substantial. Janice's father had died and, I think, left her real money, and Kyle's clinics were doing well. They had bought a lot in a subdivision on a large tract of land on the bluff over the river that had originally been given to the University of Texas. The university considered that stellar site from the point of view of its highest and best use, and so sold it to developers. It was also south of the river, but west, just over the low water crossing below the Tom Miller Dam. We drove over together to see the lot, which was huge. Kyle and Janice were clearly happy. Maya and Emily played along the dragging limb of one fantastic oak while we looked around. The new houses in the neighborhood were mostly all over-large neo-historic pastiche. It was like someone had given a group of supersized drag queens the keys to the wardrobe of a historical society.

I didn't quite get it. I looked over at Kyle: "So you see yourselves fitting in here?"

"Sure. I know a lot of the doctors living here."

"I was thinking more along the lines of the sizes and styles of these houses."

"Yeah, it's a little funky, but we need the space, and I like the fact that we can build bigger and still be close in to town."

"And the pretensions of these houses" — I pointed to a faux-mansarded mansion — "don't drive you nuts?"

"How do you mean?"

"Well, that house would be happier in the French countryside, if that countryside happened to be within the borders of Euro Disney."

"Dave," Kyle said, smiling, "other people's pretensions don't bother me at all. I mean, it's an all right house. Who cares? And come on, they're not force-feeding penned geese over there."

Janice laughed, "So don't make it French. I'm not intending to grow armpit hair ..."

"*Eeeew*, mom, so *GROSS!*" Emily had come walking back with Maya in tow. The little girl held out her hand: "Look." In her upturned palm was an almost perfect tan flint spear point. One tiny ear was broken off.

"Maya, *amazing*! Where did you find it?"

Maya pointed to the black felt silt fence along the lower edge of the neighboring lot. Contractors have to put those in during construction to keep loose topsoil, which is laced with heavy metal fertilizers, from running into the storm drains that in turn drain to the river. "It was there in the mud," Emily explained. We walked down and poked around a bit — there was a lot of broken flint, but nothing else of consequence.

Back at their house Janice showed me a notebook of photographs torn from magazines of things she liked. There were a lot of pictures of stone-walled farmhouses and country villa rooms, with wisteria and lavender growing in the background. Architects get shown those photos a lot. They were actually of beautiful spaces, but all quite formal. Janice had a floor plan she liked too. It was traditional: symmetrical, central entry hall, a great room one side, a sort of library/parlor/den the other, dining room and kitchen across the back, the bedrooms upstairs. It was an interesting plan because you could project any style onto it. But, spatially, it wasn't particularly compelling. That and the site really confused me. I couldn't figure it out. I mean, they weren't any more conservative in how they lived their lives, but all of the things they wanted were staid and conventional, without risk. But that happens sometimes because people haven't been exposed to possibilities, or don't know where to look.

I ended up proposing something I thought made more sense thinking of them as an *architect*. You could make a fairly large building footprint on their lot. I modeled that footprint as a rectangular block, imagining it as a large, simple mass of stone or plaster. Set into the slope it was a generous story and a half high on the downhill side. Into the block from above I cut a large austere rectangular courtyard (which had a small garden and a long thin lap pool). I oriented the courtyard to the true cardinal directions, which turned out to be at a slightly odd angle to the outline of the house, which sat parallel to the street. I then literally carved the rooms into the block from the courtyard. But I kept the rooms rectangular, and parallel to the courtyard, so they didn't exactly align with the outside of the mass of the house. Then, into the angled spaces available between the outer line of the rooms and the outer line of the house, I carved immense deep window openings, each of which automatically had an irregular plan. The windows were deep enough to sit in, some even to sleep in.

There were easily enough rooms to house all the different purposes. Because of the windows, each room was also a different *place* –a tall dark big room that you dropped down into on steps from the courtyard, a wide bright medium-sized room, a tiny square cell at the end of a tunnel. The house was laid out with simple circulation around the courtyard, so the purpose of each room didn't really matter. Over time, really with the exception of the kitchen, the uses of rooms could change. Between rooms there were sometimes thick walls, and sometimes sliding doors, so you could have changing sorts of privacies. I got the closets and bathrooms to work pretty easily, because you could hide those in the mass between the rooms.

It sounds complicated, but it wasn't, because of the courtyard. I loved the idea that the geometry of their family was going to be different from the geometry of that subdivision. I worked hard to perfect the design: it actually made me happy. In truth, the building was something of an ugly pet, but not all beauty is visual. The elevations of the house were conventionally misshapen, since they were just the direct result of cutting windows from the inside out. But that's actually how a lot of old farmhouses and barns obtained their order — and their charming unselfconscious appearance — and I had those in mind because those buildings were something they liked.

When I presented the design to Kyle and Janice, Kyle said "Yeah ...," then, shaking his head, "No." He actually said *no* in a way that was beautiful but almost impossible to describe. It was not so much a negation as it was an assertion of the mysterious alpha order of a family, in which he simply ranked above me. So I doubly felt I couldn't argue about it, given that it was also the only work I had. Janice I think mistook my being quiet for being upset. She said, "David, the house doesn't have to solve our problems. We just want it to stand still while we figure ourselves out." So, then, we went with their plan for a cautious house. It was a disappointment, but it didn't outweigh working on my own.

At the start of construction the builder stripped the topsoil out for the foundation of the house and piled it near the street. Dirt is a mystery: it costs you money to haul away, and again to bring it back, so you keep what you can. One day I walked past the pile just after a rain, and there were pieces of flint shining out. Some were shards, but there were three more spear points, and the long broken edge of some obscure scraping tool. I gave them to Janice. She wanted to take them over to the Texas Memorial Museum — built on the UT campus to celebrate one century of Texas — on one of the weekends they have when scientists from the university try to identify weird natural *shrap* you've found. I love that word, shrap. Emily taught it to me. "It's shit and crap combined, and you can say it in front of adults." One of the scientists said the points were Comanche, perhaps two hundred years old. He said the points found on high ground were likely tossed aside by men, as camps were typically closer to the water. Janice was pleased.

Afterward we walked around the museum. In the large mostly empty main hall there was an exhibit about the construction of the state capitol, and a gift shop, and Janice took the girls there to get some dinosaur stuff. I wandered over to a full-size plaster study for the statue of a woman that stands atop the capitol dome, holding aloft a lone star. It's pretty riveting. All of her proportions are correct, except for her face, which is frighteningly disfigured. It was designed to make sense from a distance. But up close it's truly horrid, almost melted. You can't look at it. Janice came walking up with the girls, and stopped cold: "That's just wrong." Later, after I had dropped everyone off, I drove over to the capitol. It's a beautiful building, and huge. I stood on the sidewalk in front and stared at the figure perched on top of the dome. It seemed perfect, in every respect, though it was hard to be sure at that distance.

The Honey Trap

The Honey Trap

When I moved to Austin I rented the front half of a duplex on the first ridge up from Shoal Creek, directly west of downtown, in what is called Old West Austin. The unit was mostly a walled courtyard, even to the street, with a single-story living space and bedroom running along the north side, opening onto the courtyard, and another similar unit in back. It wasn't conventionally residential, but I also needed it as an office, and it looked like an office from the street. I saw it to rent during the daytime, and didn't realize, or just did not think to realize, that at night it would never get dark, as the courtyard sat almost directly under the moonlight tower at 12th and Blanco. I didn't notice the moonlight tower at all during that first day: it was just another piece of necessary and unquestioned infrastructure, like fire hydrants or cell towers. The first night the light was really bright on the courtyard walls. I assumed it was just the full moon. A few nights in I realized the moon wasn't changing.

Austin got this unusual system of street lighting just over a hundred years ago: 31 slender towers, each about a hundred and fifty feet tall, and each with a battery of six arc lamps, which, though high,

47

produced enough silvery light to read at ground level underneath. To pay for the towers the city gave the manufacturer the right to operate a train out to the original dam at the bottom of Lake Austin, where the electricity for the lights was being generated in the first place, and where you could take steamboat rides. When the dam burst, the city was plunged into darkness for several years, and the train operator went broke. But when the new coal plant came on line the towers went back into operation.

Albany, New Orleans, and a few other cities had similar systems of lights, all assembled from kits of beautifully thought-through prefabricated cast-iron parts. Only Austin still has towers working, though their light is now obscured by many smaller street lamps. Originally the arc filaments had to be replaced daily. The open triangular truss structure of each tower housed a little basket and counterweight elevator that carried the lamp man (you had to be about as heavy as the counterweight to get the job) up to a hexagonal platform from which the lights were hung. Now the city electric company sends out a cherry picker to replace the retrofitted mercury vapor bulbs every few years. The cherry picker doesn't quite reach the platform: workmen prop a ladder across the dizzying span at the top. The original elevator didn't quite come all the way down either, stopping ten feet or so above the ground, where the triangular tower frame converges to a single column, in the hope of dissuading anyone from climbing. So, of course, climbing the towers instantly became one of the adolescent challenges of the city, like in *Dazed and Confused*.

It's a cyclical challenge at best. I remember as a kid reading that someone had fallen climbing illegally near the top of one of the towers, and, bouncing down — there was a beautiful diagram in all the Texas papers — had dislodged the electrical wires feeding the lamps. He miraculously grabbed onto one of the horizontal struts, only to have the loose wire, swaying back and forth, strike the tower, electrifying the whole thing while he dangled there, like Wiley Coyote. The poor guy survived, and recovered, only to be sued by the city. The portion of the tower where he had managed to hang on was taken down for the trial. It now sits outside the School of Architecture at UT, though the blackened handprints, which were used as evidence, are hard to discern.

One of the reasons I hadn't seen the tower in the first place was its fineness. The struts and couplings are remarkably thin, light enough to be installed by a man without heavy machinery. They get thinner in stages as the load on the tower decreases with height. The 19th-century machining is precise, as precise as the machine's task. The towers never lit the city evenly. Instead they formed a sort of overhead map. Traveling through the now pleasant dark matter in between, you could always position yourself according to the constellation of floating moons. When I'm aware of the tower light I think about what it must have been like to be a teenager in Austin when they were first lit. Can you imagine? To suddenly have, out of the inky shut-in blackness, a series of destinations — of strange attractors — to flit to no longer the world of adults, of arranged meetings in parlors or churches, but a new city of possibility, each cone of light a new sphere of discovery, where one could appear unannounced, then vanish into the shadows?

I found the duplex in an ad placed at the Architecture School. The other half was being rented by two Germans who were here as graduate students in architecture, Sabina and Axel, both of whom I eventually ended up hiring part time. They had not come to Austin together, but had met here at the university. In their peculiarly German way it was unclear if they were romantically involved. Sabina told me that she had spent some time trying to date Americans. She said, "Months long I waited for someone to ask me to go out just for a dinner. I had to ask, ultimately. I made a friend and we did things together. Right away a thing happened. Many other men started calling me on the telephone, to ask me to go out."

I told her it's the same way with work as an architect. Once you have work, more work finds you. You start emitting a respectability pheromone. Just after I'd started working on Kyle and Janice's house I got a call to design another house, for which the constitutional logic was so exact that I am, still now, in sudden unprepared moments, flushed — I can feel my ears light up — by the ruthlessness of its calculation.

The clients were from Beaumont, the heart of sweaty refinery country along the coast. That part of Texas stinks of petroleum, "the smell of money." They were retiring to Austin in their mid-sixties: Frank and Cissy — for Frances — Daniels. They'd gotten my name from Kyle's contractor. We talked on the phone, and I sent them images of Kyle and Janice's house. We had a long first meeting in Austin. At first glance Frank and Cissy seemed sanded down, ordinary in a way that's disheartening to architects. Often it means people who believe they are radical because they want to uphold the status quo, as if the status quo was somehow threatened. Cissy was dressed to seem inoffensively wealthy. Frank was groomed to disappear. I learned later they had the ability to always appear clean. I was surprised they did hire me, because right away I think we both sensed our values were not the same. But that's often true, so perhaps it was just me, worrying. Architects tend to hide their values, not wanting to offend, or perhaps its a profession attractive to the apolitical.

Frank was an electrical engineer. He'd made his money with the design and installation of the fiber optic cable matrix along the upper Texas coast. He'd argued for burying it, and put his own cash behind his claim, which had proven prescient with the big storms that then came through later. I don't know if you've had much experience with retired successful engineers, but I have yet to meet one that didn't manage — by not smiling when they should, or by just not holding up their end of a conversation — to let you know they don't quite believe your explanations. Architecture is, at heart, qualitative work — it's about the qualities of the thing you live in — but most men middle age and beyond think it's all systems, square footages, cost analysis. For me those things are down the line, after the fundamental problem is figured out.

I mean, buildings are expensive, and they happen rarely, and the process is demanding, so you might as well figure out what your deep desires are. A lot of people sense that, anyway. They build a house because, for example, there is trouble in the marriage, and they think a new house can fix it. But it's a stressful process, so usually they end up divorced. Problems can pretty well be defined by how complex their solutions are — Band-Aid, brandy, bank loan — so when you get to *building* you should be in some deep shrap.

Cissy understood. Frank had typed up a long list of bulleted items and concerns: low maintenance, lots of storage, low energy consumption, low cost — these lists are invariably the same. I glanced at it out of the corner of my eye — it included an extraordinary number of rooms for a couple that was retiring — as finally we started talking about what they were trying to accomplish.

Then it was mostly Cissy speaking, and it was a pleasure to listen to her voice. Particular to women in the wealthier classes in Texas — actually, in most of the South — there's status associated with sounding like you grew up hard-working poor in some little country town, or on a farm or ranch, so your accent and cadence — and your gracious good manners — come off as unshakably ingrained and authentic. Then you went off to get a sound liberal arts education, married smartly — not excessively — worked hard to raise a decent family and build a life, succeeded. Even if it's true, and it usually is. It isn't just the pleasing accent, or the politeness. There is a necessary component of forthright honesty in the content — "My son was struggling with alcohol then" — that comes across as humble. It's hard to describe. At first you think it's genuinely unpretentious. Then you realize it's a trained and powerful tool, the kind of thing that makes feminists despair. Anyhow, you find yourself struggling like Odysseus to disagree with anything you're being told, for the sound.

"Thirty years ago Frank and I built a house in Beaumont to raise our growing family. You will have to believe me, it was quite contemporary for the time. It even had intercoms in all the rooms. We love that house, though have come to realize it no longer makes sense for us."

"It's too big?"

"Oh, not really, I suppose. The boys have all left Beaumont, and Frank is retired. We raised four beautiful sons, but we were not blessed with daughters of our own. Two are in Dallas — Ken and Donna, and

Peter and Diana — John is in Houston, and Chris lives near San Antonio. He's married to Katie. We love Beaumont dearly and have our good friends there, but, you know, we would like to slow down. It's not the town we knew. Many of our old neighbors now live in the Hill Country, and our best friends have moved to Wimberley. Our lot is out on the Pedernales bluff, but it turns out we know quite a few folks within a half hour's drive."

As she was saying this, Frank had pulled out pictures of the site. It had a beautiful high view south over the river.

"That's a nice place. I'm assuming you want the new house to be focused on the outdoors?"

"Not exactly," Cissy continued, "though we certainly love the countryside, and it is beautiful land, and you can get right down to the river. I know you will love it too. Our house in Beaumont has a pretty yard. The trees we planted with the boys. But they don't really want to come back there anymore. I can understand that, certainly. They all have families, and their own lives."

"And is the house in Beaumont too small then?"

"David, I know you'll appreciate this when you have a family, but there comes a time when they are no longer so able to come see you very often. They have the time, but they also have such strong wives! I love those girls dearly, but you know the saying about losing sons to marriage."

"Wait I don't know. What do they say?"

"The gist of it — Frank, how does it go? — you gain a son when your daughters marry, but lose your sons to their new wives' families — something to that effect. It is hard for the boys to come back, so in some way we have lost them. Our family had its old rhythms and patterns in that house. You know how women are. The boys need to show their wives that their new lives are more important. The house is still the same as before they moved away. Just renovating can't change that! I feel the old house makes everyone feel a bit guilty when we're together, and the girls are counting the minutes. Really, it's fine — I understand and remember how that felt — I disliked going to Frank's old house too."

"Well, Cissy, I suppose we could ask your children to help design the house, or parts of it. Would that be smart? Though it sounds as if you'd like the new house to be more of a blank slate, maybe with each family having some privacy, or some part they feel is their own."

"David, the thought is right. I want them to be able to have places to get away from us, almost separate apartments, and none of it too formal. But, I should still say something else about the old house. You see, we have lovely grandchildren..."

"Grandchildren?" — I said that in just the way you would to get work.

"This may surprise you, but we have seven, and one on the way. Ken and Donna have four girls, all close together, and the last two are twins, who just had their fourth birthdays. And Chris and Katie have three, and Peter is finally starting a family. We want to see more of them, and that is really the reason we are moving to the country."

"Because it's hard for them to get to Beaumont?"

"Oh, you know, actually it isn't too hard. Chris even has work there. We worry though that the children are starting to get the sense their grandparents are no fun, because of how everyone gets along in our old house."

"Ah — I think I just got it."

"David, what I've been thinking about is what we could offer that they don't have. One thing is the countryside, and being in nature."

"Because it's innocent. Nature I mean..."

"That is part of it, you're right. We are certainly going to have to make it that way. You know, we'll have to hire someone to get rid of the fire ants. But the outdoors is a setting. The real issue is the house..." — Cissy gave me a level look — "I just want it to offer everything the kids don't get to do at home."

"Because of — but the boys must be doing reasonably well." I was trying to find a way to politely express a question that had entered my mind, about the boys' families somehow struggling financially.

Cissy understood the gist of my comment: "Oh, they are all doing fine. But they are also in the time of their lives when it is more important to put money away. They would never think to spend for horses, or a putting green or pool table, or for a raft and a rope swing into the river, or a sauna, even though I think they'll enjoy those things once they know they are available."

"The house as a — as a sort of — as a honey trap."

Cissy darkened: "I beg your pardon?"

"Well, maybe that's the wrong term. I meant it like setting out sugar to catch ants."

Cissy paused and looked at me, and for a moment I thought I had lost the job. She turned and slightly shifted a model sitting on a file cabinet next to her. Then she smiled. "You know, David, when I was a mother of young children I just let them be. They would come home from school and then check in at dinner. That's not the way now. The children are so supervised — they never have a free moment. Their mothers put so much emphasis on what is or isn't good for them, as if we never raised any! And they are never allowed to do *anything*! It is really quite stressful. I want the new house to be a place where my boys and their wives don't feel threatened by my reality, and aren't worried that their own children are indulging themselves."

"When you say indulging themselves..."

"Oh, in every way — I want each family to have its own privacy, and each bedroom to have a big bathroom, and each bathroom a big tub, and each tub with those water jets. I would love for there to be a place where all the kids can watch any movie they want, and a fireplace big enough to roast marshmallows. Perhaps there should even be a place to throw darts, or shoot a gun, or drive one of those four-wheel motorcycles — well, I suppose all those happen outside! I want the house to be full of fantasy, to look old, and for there to be flowers and a big pool, with a slide."

"You want the grandchildren to want to come..."

"Yes, that is exactly what we want. For the rest, Frank and I don't need too much. We like to eat in the kitchen. We'd like separate bathrooms..."

After Frank and Cissy left, Sabina, who'd sat in on the meeting, asked: "So, you will help them with their plot?" — though, in retrospect, it struck me she might have been referring to the piece of land.

Their site was at the edge of what is now arguably Austin, where the Pedernales River turns into Lake

Travis. It was a large flat meadow on the high bluff there, with rusted beer can pull-tabs everywhere from some ancient encampment. The first house design I presented was strung through the site, quite severe and abstract, and heavily reliant on views of the landscape, with low roofs sloping only in the directions of various views, and all of its parts connected to an open and very light steel-framed porch floating above the landscape that you could seal off in part with sail-like curtains.

But Cissy quickly put a stop to it — she wanted the house to have a far greater component of fantasy, and at the same time be more of a centralized compound, and she insisted on pitching the roofs normally, without cantilevers, but with wood-columned porches, "…as it is done correctly." It wasn't really something you could reasonably object to, the way Cissy made her limits clear. So the design closed down a bit: it became well mannered, and un-demanding, hardly really architecture. But, as I said, I was happy for the work, and Cissy was astonishing to work with. Everything was pinned down exactly.

Not surprisingly, construction proceeded smoothly enough, with one odd exception. When we were deciding major colors for the painted parts of the house just before actual building started, Cissy started making uncharacteristically bad choices: a lurid bright purple, an almost safety-glow orange. The colors were interesting, but wrong. Even Frank objected – it was his primary input – but Cissy remained firm. Months later, when we were two weeks into painting, which happens towards the end of construction, I got a sweet call from Cissy. She'd just had cataract surgery, and realized what she thought was lavender was not. Could I get the painters to start over?

I drove out to the house, but none of the painters were in it, though I'd passed all of their cars coming along the entry drive. Eventually I found the whole crew slumped inside one of their vans, with their heads down. The crew chief got out and walked over to me, and from the redness of his eyes I could see that he had either been weeping or smoking dope — with painters it's hard to tell. I asked what was going on. "Oh man, *Jerry Garcia* died!" I told them to take the rest of the day off, and we'd start fresh.

As construction began to wrap up there came a point where Cissy asked me to help her obtain certain things she wanted for the house. She had me get in touch with Donna, Ken's wife in Dallas, to get an idea of the kinds of toys and sundries that it made sense to plan storage for. I spent a day in Dallas, and we ended up buying — beyond a lot of furniture — a telescope, several pairs of binoculars, field guides for animals, birds, butterflies, and trees, bug boxes, croquet mallets, hammocks, inner tubes, life jackets, and so on. In the process I got to know Ken and Donna — lovely easy-going competent people, as Cissy had said.

When the house was done Frank and Cissy threw a big party. Ken and Donna picked me up in Austin on their way down from Dallas to drive out to the house in their Suburban. Past Dripping Springs the road had been recently repaved and it was a supremely pleasant drive, just a continuous white hissing noise uninterrupted by seams or patching. There must have once been a set of road engineers in Texas dedicated to a kind of high-speed Zen: Ken could almost drive without his hands, the momentum of the vehicle being perfectly redirected in the curves and dips. The four girls had managed to pack themselves in the very back seat of the Suburban, with the twins double-buckled in the middle. Every now and then I would turn to look at them from where I was sitting alone in the middle row, and I could hear them happily attending to themselves, singing and flittering to each other's passing whims.

We came over a rise and before us the road traced a long parabola down into a wash and up the drainage to the rolling crest beyond, perhaps a quarter mile. At the top of the far slope, in the right lane, a squirrel was nosing something on the road. There was a sudden concerned silence from the girls in the back, and I turned around to see eight very round eyes staring intently at the squirrel that the Suburban was now barreling toward, and four little mouths equally round drawing in air sharply.

Coming through the dip and climbing up the other side, Ken gradually brought the Suburban into the oncoming lane in a long swerve. But now the squirrel moved in little stutters left over the centerline into our path, so Ken brought the truck back over to the right. The squirrel continued onto the far shoulder, but then, just as we passed, it shot back across the road as if demonically possessed, directly under the truck. It may have missed the front wheels, but it was definitely caught by the back: you could feel the little furry bump on that smooth road. I turned around just as the four girls' heads swiveled synchronously back, like the tracking device for a laser-guided bomb. Between the twins I could see back down the road. The squirrel came into view. It seemed to get up — at least its tail suddenly stood straight up — but then it keeled over, obviously dead. I was mortified for the girls, as their googly eyes slowly found each other again. And then, as if one, the girls erupted: "*YYYYESSSS!!!*" A crazed hilarity took over back there, as the girls began high-fiving each other, and pumping their fists: "*YES!!*"

The party went off nicely. The wives seemed happy with the arrangements. Late in the afternoon I found the twins sleeping in front of a television. Some months later I happened to be speaking with Cissy, and asked about how the house was working. She told me a sad thing had happened. The ornamental rose bushes she had planted had attracted deer. Frank had set out deer feeders, but little could keep the deer from destroying the plantings, so Frank had started shooting deer from the house — "It was that or name them." This, it turned out, was simple to do. Between two of the guest suites there was a little terrace you could get to directly from the pool without disturbing anyone. Frank would get up before dawn, make coffee, carry it out to the terrace, position the rifle in the dark, wait for the sun to come up, then pull the trigger, all without ever getting out of his bath robe. Since many of the deer were Axis, an introduced species, there wasn't a limit — anyway, there are more deer in the Hill Country now than ever in recorded history.

For some weeks Frank had been taking deer into Dripping Springs to be processed into steaks and sausage. The meat was fantastic, so lean you had to add grease to the pan. Cissy had sent a freezer box of the best backstrap steaks to Ken and Donna in Dallas. Two days later she got a call from Donna, who read her the riot act over the phone, saying the girls were mortified, horrified — just shy of permanently damaged — and it would be some time before they could come back. But things were hopeful. Ken and Donna had spent a week out at the house while Frank and Cissy had been away. Cissy had found little notes hidden throughout the house, from the girls, telling her how much they loved her.

A Life in Ruins

A Life in Ruins

Every year the AIA — the professional organization for architects — sponsors a tour of new houses in Austin to promote architecture. On that day you get to invade a lot of privacy, arguably to get a sense of what's going on. But, really, it's not critics along for the ride, it's all voyeurs. The AIA gives you a map, and you drive along from one house to the next. The architects are usually there, and the clients too, and sometimes even the builders — in some houses you can still smell the wet paint. In the morning there might be some serious questions about content, but mostly it's the middle-aged appreciating kitchen layouts, or improvements in plumbing technology. The year I went one of the houses had a remote control toilet from Japan that you flushed with something like a TV clicker, to avoid the aeration of bacteria — or to torture your significant other. I think of it every time I flush now, and it tempers my bathroom with dissatisfaction and worry.

The tour, it's the kind of thing I hate. I would prefer to wait until the owners are dead. I only went because some clients, Paul and Shelly Delveccio, wanted me to accompany them. Paul was a tech industry wizard who'd made a fortune with a product he had developed and marketed called *Honestly!*, a sort of home polygraph. *Honestly!* came with face and arm sensors — clad in brightly colored foam — you attached to your computer, the idea being that you'd strap in your friends and ask them all sorts of embarrassing questions. Originally the information was transmitted to a server, the results read out in real time on your computer screen. Now it was all handled by straight-up software. *Honestly!* was somewhat subversively advertised as a children's game. It's real success was as a parenting tool and an adult party toy. Paul had sold enough to never have to work again, and he wasn't, and neither was Shelly, who had quit her work as a lawyer.

Instead, they were both being parents of three young children, and fully diving into things that interested them. Just then the thing was building the ultimate house, a project to which they brought a frightening concentration. The project consisted of two parts. There was the house itself, which we'd been going round and round about. They wanted it to be like a castle — and they weren't compromising for an "interpretation" of a castle, either. They wanted turrets, and hidden passageways, and lots of stone.

Then there was the complex reclamation of the land, which they hoped to return to a pre-settler state. The eighty acres they had purchased, once a goat farm, were isolated, out near Pedernales Falls. So that was a huge undertaking, trying to revitalize springs by clearing cedar, and restarting grassland, which isn't just about leaving things alone, but requires extraordinary care, work, and money. It also requires the removal of established invader species, which has its interesting limits, since you have to decide how far back you want to set the clock.

We talked a lot about why they were making the move, and Shelly mentioned this useful thing: "You know, we feel our lives are filled with false socialization — in meeting rooms, and elevators, and cocktail parties. Also, we're tired of the competitiveness. I took Jane for an interview at a church day school, and the kid before us could already tie his shoes. Jane took the poor boy's little stuffed toy and wouldn't give it back, and, honestly, I felt like the teachers were thinking: you are such a lousy mom!"

Despite the seeming incongruity of their desires, we got along easily. Early on, when we were discussing various locations for the house, they had wanted to be on-site all day for several days, and so they had asked me to camp with them at a nearby state park. They timed the trip to coincide with the Perseid meteor shower. I got there just after dark, and had to stumble over from the car to where they had set up portable lounge chairs to watch the night sky. I'd assumed the campground was relatively empty, but when a meteor arced over, you could hear people up and down the valley yelling and whooping, like at a UT football game. In the morning I woke up in my tent to an odd hissing sound. I looked out, but no one was up yet. The hiss seemed to be coming from Paul and Shelly's tent. I put on my shoes and walked over there. All you could see was a hundred-foot extension cord running back to a power outlet where the cars were parked. Paul stuck his bearded head out his tent zipper: "Cappuccino?" Needless to say I liked them a lot.

Anyhow, on the morning of the AIA tour I was late to get to the first house because I felt compelled to free an armadillo caught inside a live trap I'd set in my courtyard. Several weeks earlier I had woken up to find an armadillo rooting through the garden in the courtyard of my duplex. An armadillo is like Leonardo had consented to design a military plow. I had tried to catch it in a trashcan, but armadillos are enormously quick once they sense your presence, and it shot off behind a row of bushes and vanished. Looking where it went I found and promptly filled a hole burrowed under the wall. Two days later the armadillo was back plowing, so I bought a live trap and set it under the run in the bushes, first aimed one way, then the other, until finally I found it inhabited the morning of the tour.

There was still time before I had to meet Paul and Shelly, so I lugged the caged armadillo to the back of my car, with the intention of transporting it to the park on Red Bud Isle just below the Tom Miller Dam. The canyon of the Colorado constricts there handsomely, and it was the logical first spot along the unpredictable river to be dammed. When the original dam, the one that powered the moonlight towers, silted up and burst, its ruins formed islands just downstream (you can still see fragments of the structure), at the top of Town Lake. That area is the park. It can exist because Lake Austin and Town Lake both have constant water levels, their shoreline inhabitants having more political clout than the dirt farmers farther downstream. People fish there for perch and bass — apparently there are really large bass. The discharge from the dam aerates the water, so the fish are narced up. You aren't supposed to eat the fish because of PCB's in the river from an old power station downtown, so mostly you see fly fishermen catch-and-releasing. Once a year there is (or was) supposedly a strange nighttime rowing regatta that starts from Red Bud: I've heard all the rowers are naked, or nearly so.

As I was driving, I was thinking there are now a lot of animals in Austin. Maybe there have always been, but I don't think so. White-winged doves, which were human shy when I was a kid, seem to have flocked to the city, perhaps discovering its relative safety. I've seen alligator lizards and all kinds of snakes, and hawk and kite migrations over the city, and countless warblers and raccoons, and possums, those post-nuclear rats. How animals work out their patterns of existence in the urban frame is a mystery to me. Do they find what they know to work, or do they adjust?

The most improbable example here is the colony of bats under the Congress Avenue Bridge, which carries the main axis of the city across Town Lake to the south shore. The bridge was restructured in 1980 using prefabricated concrete beams, the spacing and profile of which turned out to be just right for Mexican free-tailed bats to roost. I don't know how long it took for the bats to discover the bridge, but there is now a huge breeding colony there from late spring through early fall. At dusk the bats pour out from under the bridge in a cloudy stream, and the crowd of people that wait every evening for this amazing sight usually applaud. It's thickest in late summer, when the young bats are weaned and add to the flight. In the morning the bats return, and the rowers on the lake see them plummet out of the sky like rocks.

The road on which I was driving to Red Bud Isle drops steeply to the river, then flattens jarringly as the road passes over a series of concrete fins about an eighth of a mile below the dam. Just as I came down hard onto that stretch I noticed, in the rearview mirror, the armadillo, which had somehow freed itself from the trap, leaping up and slamming itself against the ceiling of the hatch. The leaping instinct of armadillos is what kills them on roads. They jump up into the undercarriage of cars just as they pass.

I pulled off the road into the parking lot on Red Bud Isle and sprinted around to open the hatch, but that action frightened the armadillo over into the folded-down back seat. I opened all the doors and tried to bully the damn thing out with a roll of drawings, but instead it wedged itself under the front seat, from which it could not be dissuaded. My heart was racing, and I stepped away from the car to breathe. I mean, armadillos are harmless, but still I found it unnerving. Finally, decided, I reached in and grabbed it by the tail, pulled, and heaved it over into the grass. The creature's toenails left furrows in the floor mat. Having grass underfoot seemed to calm it down, and it just ambled off. I stood there sweating, listening to the armadillo shuffling its way through the leaves down to the shore.

The armadillo had urinated and defecated throughout the back of the car. To be sure, there was an aeration of bacteria. All I had to clean it with was a T-shirt I had on underneath the corduroy dress shirt I was wearing. After I'd wiped up as much as I could I walked down to the shore to rinse the T-shirt and wring it out. From there you could see a group of kayakers that had paddled up to the spume below the raceway of the dam's power plant, where they were practicing full rolls, flopping sideways into the white water. A kingfisher flew by, rattling.

When I got back to the car there was a park police officer looking at the live trap in the back.
She asked: "Did you release a wild animal here?"
"Is that a problem, officer?" — I tried to explain what I'd just gone through. I was sweating again.

"It's illegal to even catch them. If you're having trouble with an animal you should call the city" — she tried to give me a card, but my hands held the dripping shirt, so she put it on the dash — "our website explains the various rules for dealing with animals. Also, just so you know, raccoons and armadillos cover a lot of ground. Releasing them here doesn't mean much, especially if they have litters." She leaned into the back of the car and sniffed.

It took a while to finish the cleanup. By now I was really late, sweaty, and driving the stinking car way too fast. Paul and Shelly had left the first house, a huge ranch house-like thing in limestone that was based on taking a cedar chopper's cabin and feeding it growth hormones. At least I got to wash up there, which is where I encountered the Japanese toilet. They had also already passed through the second house, composed of a series of little rural volumes — one metal-clad silo housed a hot tub — artfully arranged around the site in a way that made me shudder.

I caught up with them at the third house, a vaguely Italianate stucco and stone pile in the hills. As part of their house project Paul and Shelly had gone looking at villas in Tuscany, and I wondered what they would think. The grounds were all xeriscaped with beautiful native trees and grasses, not a cedar in sight. The house was disposed about an inner courtyard on the uphill side, where there was a fountain in the form of an artificial natural spring. I found Paul just off the courtyard in the public rooms, which faced north out over the river. He was locked in a somewhat heated debate with the overdressed architect about whether the porch to the courtyard was or was not correctly called a loggia.

I wandered away and finally found Shelly upstairs in the big master bedroom, which, to my utter astonishment, was — other than the presence of a very large bed — organized and decorated like a Shaker meeting room. Set symmetrically in the wall facing the bed were two tall wood-and-glass doors that let out to a terrace. Between these doors, exactly opposite the bed, was a Shaker bench. On either side of the bed were doors, one leading in from the hall, the other, apparently, leading to a bathroom and closets. The two flanking walls were also lined with Shaker benches, each bench at least sixteen feet long, extending the full width of the room. The walls were whitish plaster. A pegged wooden strip ran around the room at eye level, hung with simple adornments: a small mirror on a leather cord, white cotton bathrobes. An ab-roller was resting over two of the pegs.

Everything was done in solid cherry, beautifully dovetailed. The floor was all in cherry too, heavily figured wide boards that were either reclaimed or distressed.

Shelly was sitting on the far side of the bed. At its foot was a great Shaker chest. She had just pushed a peg in the headboard, and a TV was rising up out of the chest.

"This I like," she said, getting up and walking over to me.

I was still trying to get a grip on the room.

"I like Shaker. It is both abstract and homey."

"Shelly," I said, "It's a Shaker *master bedroom*."

She looked at me, waiting for me to finish the thought.

"Shakers didn't have sex. That's why they *shook*."

She looked around the room, then smiled: "Well, I'm sure *some* of them did, and if they'd done it more often we would have some Shakers around to build us decent furniture."

As she was saying this, a group came in from the hallway, carrying champagne in glasses — a clean silvery man in his early sixties wearing a black silk sports shirt, a forty-ish worked-on blonde woman accompanied by what one could only hope were her augmented breasts, and a tall thin man in linen who clearly had some sort of privileges because he was smoking — *he was actually smoking in the house* — a brown menthol cigarette. Introductions being made, these turned out to be the owners, the Schmidts, and their decorator, Ben Cunningham.

I was trying to place his name, when he asked, smiling thinly and feigning mock horror, "You're not one of those *modern* architects, are you?" — then, not pausing for a reply, "Don't we love the surprise of this room?"

"Shocking!" was all I could manage to reply, but Shelly overrode me politely: "This is a lovely space. It must mean a lot to you. I'm guessing it must have been inspired by something important."

This seemed to brighten Mr. Schmidt: "We spent part of our honeymoon in Shaker country up in Kentucky, near where my wife's family is from. Do y'all know it? It's one of the most beautiful places I've ever been. There's something about that way of life we find simple, and really authentic." He turned to his wife: "Honey, what was the name of that place?"

"Pleasant Hill. You must visit the inn there. All the rooms and furniture are original Shaker. So tranquil, so real. We were quite taken with it, and flew Ben…" — now I recognized his name: he'd made a fortune in Dallas transforming suburban houses into Country Homes — "…out to join us. We thought at first this whole house could be Shaker, but in the end we decided a Tuscan house made more sense here in Austin. We wanted the house to be right for this landscape we so love." She pointed to the doors leading out to the porch, through which you could see the tops of oak trees leading up a little draw. "This is our little bit of paradise, here in paradise. Ben suggested we buy the land in the view, so there will never be anything but nature. And he did such a brilliant job with the interiors of this house. It is his masterpiece."

"Thankfully, I am immune to flattery!" Ben said, clearly flattered. He paused for two beats, beaming. "Now, David, you might, as an architect, appreciate this." He walked over to a wall and, looking at me, took a puff off his cigarette, then turned and exhaled smoke in a thin stream at the peg strip. The smoke promptly blew straight up the wall. He swiveled back and announced: "No visible air supply!"

Shelly and I went over to look. The peg strip was set just off the wall, and behind it ran a thin air diffuser slot.

"Amazing," Shelly murmured.

"Let me tell you what's amazing," Ben continued,

"The Shakers did not have *architects* at all" — the guy was slamming me like a real professional — "they just knew what was right. And, of course, they didn't have electricity. Where are the outlets?"

We looked around, following the sweep of Ben's hands. "*Per favore!*" he exclaimed, walking over to a large knot in one of the cherry floorboards. He knelt down and pushed on the knot, which popped out to expose a convenience outlet. That, I admit, was cool.

"And where do you suppose the *lights* are?" We looked up, and sure enough, nothing. Ben had moved back to the bed, where he turned another Shaker peg. Apparently this was a dimmer. As he cranked it, bright white light washed up the walls from a narrow reveal between the floor and the baseboards, passing behind the bench seats, which turned out to also be set off the walls. The effect was to make the floor float, like a life raft, with the benches as a kind of safety rail.

"Wow!" Shelly said, "How do you change the bulbs?" Mr. Schmidt laughed.

Ben walked over to one of the benches, and tilted it forward. The whole floor under the bench rotated with it, revealing the light fixtures, as well as a built in vacuum cleaner fitting: "*Ecco!*"

"Nice," I said, thinking I had him, "but how do you read in bed?"

"*Reading?*" Ben was on the spot.

But Mr. Schmidt interrupted with a champagne grin: "We don't do a lot of reading." He winked at his wife.

It was a sort of Caligula moment. I certainly couldn't think of the right thing to say — like, "So, Ben, how did you solve the Viagra storage problem?" — but, with the seconds ticking away, I felt I had to say something: "Well, this is one kinky room."

"Hmm. Kinky," Ben said slowly, "that must be an *architectural* term?" He really was a patronizing genius.

"I'm sorry, that was a bad choice of words."

"I see. You *chose* those words!"

I looked at Mrs. Schmidt: "Listen, I don't know how to say this without it sounding wrong, so please don't take offense. This is a splendid room in a way, but I was wondering if you don't find it somehow very odd — I mean as a bedroom?"

"Odd?" She was looking at me blankly. You could see the pleasantness drain from her face, and sense her husband's nostrils flare.

Ben's eyebrows were way up, and he stepped in protectively, "I'm sure we're not certain what you mean. Are you referring to the Italianate space in the majority of the home?"

I was sweating again. "No, you know, this being the bedroom, with that whole Shaker abstinence thing." I tried laughing as I said this, but it had no effect other than to provoke a profound silence in the room. It was clearly going badly, and I looked over imploringly to Shelly for help, but her too-big grin told me I was on my own.

So there was no way to back out of it. "Look, I just meant that when the Shakers developed this kind of space they weren't thinking about its style. Maybe I'm wrong, but didn't they just want to have everything be real? You know, solid matter, made by hand, solving only the direct problem, because they didn't believe in appearances. So, for them, looking Shaker was a contradiction. You had to be a Shaker, and part of that was, you know, refraining from enjoying — what's the word? — *earthly* relationships."

"What ever do you mean?" Ben asked. He was completely relaxed. It was amazing to watch him work. "And what is that on your pants?"

I looked down at a smear of armadillo shit. Oh well: "Let me take another crack at it. I'm assuming from what you've got going outside, that what you like about living here, I mean in Austin, is the sense that things are pretty much real — you know, the hills, the springs, live oaks, you name it. Everyone loves that quality of this landscape — that's why they want to move here from places like Houston and Dallas. So why would you want to undercut that with this fantasy inside a fantasy?"

"Why? Because *we* are *adults!*" was Ben's triumphant reply.

For some time no said anything, waiting for me to speak. But I was beaten. Then Ben put his arms around the Schmidts, and finished me off: "Well, I am sure we'd all love to see *your* work!"

I fled, pulling Shelly along, but could hear their laughter all the way down the grand stairs. When we were finally out, Shelly put her hand on my shoulder and said, pleasantly, "You are such an *alien*! I guess in architecture school they teach you to go ahead and dig a deeper hole."

Paul was leaning on my car, and as we walked up he pointed to the mess in the back. "What the hell happened here?"

"Welcome to my world," was all I could manage.

The rest of the afternoon was a blur, with Paul and Shelly in high spirits. So in the end they got their castle, and the stream is flowing on their re-authenticated land, and Paul and Shelly go out and map the nesting sites of endangered golden-cheeked warblers. Here's what I have decided. They are making their own Eden on Earth, and they will not be expelled from the Garden, because they are writing their own ground rules. The first of these is: appearance is a reality unto itself, without recourse to things that really occur. They are conservationists, though they are destroying a hope many architects secretly harbor, that architecture is a conduit to the real.

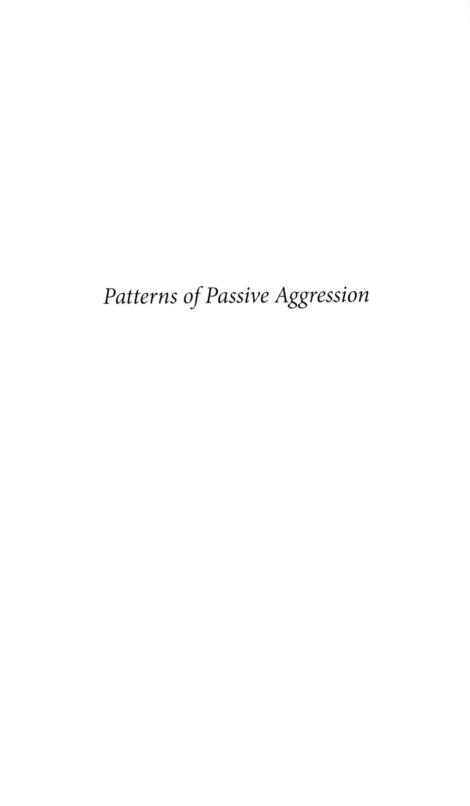

Patterns of Passive Aggression

Patterns of Passive Aggression

Late one Friday I went with a group of architects — it was a professional subgroup of *young architects* — to eat barbecue at the Salt Lick outside Austin. Inside there was a large group of University of Texas alumni. They were clearly from Dallas, as their clean, buffy men wore starched pink or ivory linen shirts with crease-ironed blue jeans over orangish boots made with expensive skins, not for working. The Salt Lick serves mostly meat and sides, you bring alcohol. The food is pretty good, but the long low dark hall with the eating porch (plastic-wrapped in winter) running along the south side is artful. There are memorably big yellow tables, well finished. It's difficult to affix the age and provenance of any of it, but it wasn't thrown together by *hicks*.

Even better is the drive out from town to get you in the mood. Once you're up onto the plateau there are weeping clear streams you pass over, little ranchettes, a two-mile stretch of highway adopted (its trash picked up) by Hill Country Nudists, the dome of the Barsana Dham temple, and then the climbing, rose-draped worm fence and lights of the stone Salt Lick buildings coming up like a roadhouse as you're dropping down to the densening woodlands of the first river cut. The Salt Lick is tended, a quality Texans admire.

The impressive thing about that group from Dallas — there were maybe sixteen young couples at a single long table — was that rather than bringing beer (everyone else was drinking beer), they'd brought tequila, which they were rapidly turning into frozen margaritas in electric blenders. There were four or five of these set at regular intervals along the table, like kinetic floral arrangements, churning intermittently, at a formal dinner. The blenders had been gang-rigged to a single industrial-grade extension cord — it had the apparent heft of rigid conduit — that ran the length of the table, then on down the restaurant, duct-taped to the floor, to the available plug, a rigorous solution to a worthwhile dilemma. There were several canvas tote bags on the floor at one end of the table, inside which you could see cardboard blender boxes, and electrician's tape and wire strippers, and more tequila, like the kit of some alcoholic yuppie burglar.

I was sitting opposite a Tom something, a young architect. He was easier to talk to when you didn't have to look at him. Tom was a pretty good-looking man, but he wore his glasses in this manner peculiar to architects that drives me to distraction. It wasn't enough for Tom to just wear glasses. The glasses had to be the evident product of design, and his were a fine clinical steel, narrow and attenuated, each joint celebrated with tiny stainless steel hex-head screws, and little German oval lenses held free along arching steel eyebrows. Fetishized, they perched on his face like a sort of mechanical praying mantis.

The effect entailed one of those weird forest-for-the-trees trade-offs that architects seem so often to make with objects, and furniture, and buildings in landscape, always shading to favor the presence of the *thing*. I suppose the glasses were extraordinary. But I just couldn't relax in their presence. I'd be looking at Tom, my focus shifting from face to glasses and back again. The whole time I was worrying: *is he looking at me looking at his glasses?*

Then there were the other young architects, who, in truth, had entered an age where their moles were sprouting hair. It takes a while to get going in this profession. There is a quality of conversation peculiar to architects, a never letting go. After an hour of drinking you could not sense any loosening had taken place with the group — though, that said, a drunk architect is usually pathetic. The conversation had started as a sort of nit-picking at the work of famous architects, but had settled on a theme about which architects like to commiserate. Architects think people aren't interested in buildings anymore, and don't look at them, and consequently don't, can't, appreciate what architects really want to do, which is to make fetishized constructions to sit on the landscape like mechanical praying mantids, which will make people look at them some more.

That's what the conversation was about. I just think the topic totally misses the point. Nobody *ever* really looks — or looked — at buildings by and large, because most buildings are of a class of things that people pay a different kind of attention to. It is precisely the not-being-noticed that I like about buildings. So, for me, the conversation was not really going anywhere. I was sitting at the window end of the table, and my mind kept drifting outside. There were white-crowned sparrows flitting through the trumpet vine growing along under the eaves: you could see their crown stripes clearly in the late light.

The food kept coming for an hour and a half, and despite an apparent mild disdain on the young architects' part it all vanished. I got up to stretch — it felt like I was carrying barbecue into the third term — and wandered outside. People were clumped under the trees, waiting for tables. The trees, all cedar elms, were unfortunately strung with tiny white Christmas lights. The restaurant had hired a singer to play the guitar and calm the hungry with cowboy-tumbleweed-Prozac songs. His voice was burry but undarkened, rising and falling in pitch but not volume, optimistic, anesthetic, a television personality for grade-school children. He had a laptop that synthesized his guitar and added rhythm and atmospherics: *clip-clop, clippity-clop.*

Cars kept coming in. A lot of the trucks had Christmas wreaths on their grills. Out in the parking lot there was a standoff between two Suburbans, over a close-in parking space. One of the Suburbans was angled into the space, but needed to back out and re-enter, which the second Suburban was refusing to allow. Isn't it always the second car that should have gotten the space? In any event the family of the second Suburban had quickly jumped out to submit their name for a table. The first family was hostage in its vehicle, pretty much pinned between a parked car and the broad nose of the second Suburban, the driver of which held them there a bit before backing off and driving on.

I went back inside and rejoined my table, but sat down nearer the big group of Dallasites. They were getting on pretty famously, having been at the margaritas now for a bit. Blenders kept firing up along the line, and a similar buzzing energy filled the conversation. Little groups were bent toward each other: there was a lot of continuous anticipatory laughter, and you could see the slight and pleasant strain on speakers' faces from willing each story into outlandishness. They seemed a happy group, competitively so, insulated from the concerns or curiosity of the other eaters.

One thing got me though. I don't know if you have ever been to Dallas, or been out in Dallas, but no one ever *relaxes* there. Dallasites work hard, and they are ever vigilant to convey seamless outward control. To their credit, they appear to believe this quality arises from the superior organization of their own private belongings, as in a correct taxonomy of personal effects. Carrying the secret knowledge of their orderly closets at home, people in Dallas are publicly enabled, as others are by wearing erotic underwear under business attire.

So I reasoned the blender people were re-living times spent in Austin. You see that a lot here, and you hear it mistily: "God, that was a *great four years*." I think many people want to come to Austin to be fundamentally irresponsible after the drudge of high school and before the drudgery of work. For a while there was a rumor floating around that UT had the highest incidence, for a big state school, of HIV among heterosexual students. I don't think it's true, but it gets to a kind of point: those kids aren't necessarily stupid, but while they're here they're happy dumb.

Actually, no one in Texas thinks of Austin as a real city, and as a city it's a model of nothing. Invented almost from scratch as the capital, its consequent slight grandeur of scale has never been matched by its industry, and so it has long had a vague, pleasant lithium quietness. Few cities — Madrid and DC come to mind — share this peculiar birthright. Like these, Austin had for many years the blessing of a constant artificial economy — the university, the government — without real boom or bust beyond the murk of real estate speculation, a city without the vagaries of city-ness. Then, really in the last fifteen years, that particular disembodied quality became desirable.

Austin arose as a city from the desire of the young nation *Texas* — having pulled off a stunningly opportunistic land grab — *we'll just get rid of the landlord* — and singularly effective public relations coup — *we'll call it freedom from tyranny* — to legitimize itself correctly. The new town was named for Stephen F. Austin, the original developer of the whole Texas concept, who secured, from the Mexican government, the initial lease allowing forty American families to virally infect the once-forbidden territory. There is still to the city the residue of both the darker underbelly and the idealistic impulse. In my mind it's not so clear that a lot of students having sex while studying isn't somehow dead on.

Pinned over my desk is a copy of an early map of Austin. The perfect rectangle of the city is well over to the eastern edge of the document. Mostly you see the Colorado River, as yet unconstrained, bending through the territory — east, then south, then east again into what will become Town Lake, out of the hills over rapids (the Deep Eddy), then along the bottom edge of the city, and away into the Blackland Prairie. Just southwest of the city grid a creek enters the river at an elbow, and perhaps a half-mile up this creek there is an area a little larger than a city block, surrounded by a fence. Within the fence there's a farmhouse, and then this sort of navel, with a little umbilical cord snaking to the creek.

That navel is Barton Springs, one of the perfect places: 23 million gallons of clear limestone-filtered water, every day, flowing from a series of cracks in the fault running along the eastern edge of the Edwards Plateau in a line extending through the state from San Antonio through New Braunfels, San Marcos, Austin, Temple, almost to Waco — Interstate-35, on the road map, traces it. Each of those towns has its springs also, where a river sutures the immense limestone sponge of the plateau to the fertile eastern farmland, and most of these oases have been inhabited for thousands of years. And on that map of Austin there is, dotted as if by little feet, a trail leading from town rather quickly out to the springs.

Barton Springs is the great psychic heart of Austin, more central, though disembodied, than the Capitol building. This is partly due to the quality of its elixir-like water, which is perpetually 67 degrees and literally stunning: when you get in and when you get out you are always *thankful*. You can swim there year-round, though some people prefer to swim in the winter, when the water doesn't seem as cold, and there is no admission charge. The week just prior to the Salt Lick dinner had started quite warm, warm enough to swim. I was floating on my back in the deeper end of the springs as a cold front came through, the temperature dropping over fifteen minutes, and the increasing wind denuding the pecan trees. Leaves floated down and gradually covered the water, and me in it.

During the Depression the creek bed along Barton's was dammed to make a swimming pool about a third of a mile long. The creek itself was channeled past the pool, under a sidewalk, so that instead the pool fills with water only from the springs. The pool is a long, thin, slightly flaring rectangle, pinched just about halfway along its length. Its long edges are partly the natural limestone creek bed and partly concrete sidewalks. The actual basin changes depth abruptly where it pinches in the center, at a series of boulders below which the springs have scoured out the channel. Fish congregate at the boulders, and occasionally in the late afternoon you see cormorants chasing fish below you, if you wear goggles. There are no lanes, but I've never run into anyone, even swimming full out.

In the variety of spaces surrounding the pool is played out — to the extent it can since you have to pay admission during the summer — a sort of map of a good part of the society of the city. Where the limestone shelf eases into the shallows next to the meadow below the bathhouse are young families and committed couples. As you move toward the middle of the pool, below the entrance, you begin to find serious regulars, who especially covet the low wall mid-pool, and the steep lawn behind it (good for winter sun), just in front of which the lap swimmers turn, or stop, and come dripping out of the cold. Across the way, framed by substantial cottonwood trees, is the diving board, home to teens and other exhibitionists. The big meadow under the pecan trees is mostly college-age singles and hipsters. Directly across the deep water, among a series of thin and fractured retained areas, you will find individualists and isolationists of every stripe. Within the wide open-air dressing rooms people sometimes sunbathe naked.

The short sides of the pool at the far ends are sidewalk-thick dams. The dam upstream looms over the shallows. Downstream, hidden by the deep water, the dam is an invisible lip dropping to the creek bed beyond. Dogs and kids and adults congregate there to play in the free runoff turbulence. So, when you float or swim in the deep, or look along the pool from the shallow end, you can't see the creek immediately below the lower dam. Instead your eye is channeled along the densely wooded valley, which points more or less directly back toward the city. Since the trees hide low-lying chaff, near or far, for many years there was nothing much to see in the distance.

Then, in 1973, American Bank built a skyscraper on the block at Colorado and 6th, exactly central to that view. The building was covered with reflective gold-tinted glass, the use of which dates a building more unambiguously than any Carbon-14 test ever could. As the sun went down, that golden tower twinkled like the onset of a migraine headache for every swimmer in the cold water. I recall reading or hearing somewhere that Heidegger said the *site* for a building was a lance as it glittered in the sun, symbolizing intent, or as it was thrust into the earth, symbolizing presence. It wasn't hard to get the gist that, for many Austinites, the bald fact of the bank tower awakened the sinking realization that sinister forces were afoot, ones which had designs upon the city that perhaps did not include making still more perfect the methods of floating in the springs between bouts of sex, studying, governing, or blending margaritas.

And, of late, the Springs are increasingly being closed following big rains, when the fecal coliform count jumps too high. Development of the vast emptiness upstream and to the west is thought to be a culprit. Gray water is sometimes used to irrigate golf courses over the recharge zone, which reaches out toward Bee Cave, where another Austin begins around and about Lake Travis. The presence of a salamander endemic to the Springs was used to try to slow that development; in turn it was used by developers to try to prevent swimming. Facts, politics, money: the Springs are gradually being strangled, as one landscape takes over another, like starlings, or hydrilla, or antibiotic-resistant strep.

The Monday following the dinner at the Salt Lick I got an apparently benign phone call, about building a house out at Lake Travis, from a man named Gordon Maggers. The conversation really didn't click, and I was put off by it. Mostly I thought he would be a client who would never get the value of working with an architect, so probably would hate paying. But it was hard to tell. Gordon kept jumping into his explanations mid-way, assuming I understood, because of what he thought architects did. I started talking about normal services, and billing, and the design process, but he cut me off. He was already somewhere else: "No, no — I know how the house is going to be laid out. I already have plans, they need some changes."

"But, you don't know how it's going to look?"

"No, I do, it's a traditional house. I saw it at Lakeway, and I have pictures. I talked to the owner, and those are the plans I have, from that builder."

So — wait — you just need it redrawn? But mainly you're looking for ... a contractor? I mean, can't that builder make it for you?"

"Well, yes and no. He can, but there's just an unusual thing, about where it has to go. The builder said maybe I should talk to an architect, or maybe an engineer. I think you could understand it out there better. Certainly I could explain it to you more clearly. Look, could I just pay you to come out for half the day?"

The next morning I drove out the Southwest Parkway, then along 71, roughly paralleling Barton Creek, turning in at Bee Cave, where 620 runs north to the Mansfield Dam, which forms Lake Travis. Lake Travis is the anti-Springs: all beer and melanoma, and overlarge portions, and people being killed in powerboats, and *Home Owners' Rights*. The lake is about 60 miles long, its shoreline an aggressive, expanding exurb. Despite the water, it's hard to imagine dwelling there. The landscape is largely barren, depressing, like an irrigation project. The waterline varies in elevation over the year, to maintain the constant water level of

Lake Austin downstream. To get insurance and permits, house builders have to set finish floor levels at least one foot above the highest possible flood line. So all the houses sit like flotsam at that elevation, lined up short on short side, just above a bathtub ring of dead black sticks and bits of styrofoam.

Actually the water only rarely reaches that high line. Below is all washed gunmetal gray limestone, and whatever ferocious plantlings seed fast enough between floodings, and shards of brown glass. Shoreline lot owners watch this moonscape — it's the bulk of their property — appear and disappear as the water level rises and drops over the hundred or so feet it will vary. Even above the flood line the soil is scarce. The trees are stunted, the houses severely exposed. At least, set by the waterline, they are out of each other's view.

I turned west off 620 onto a fresh blacktop separating hilltop lots to the left and waterfront lots to the right. From the position of the houses on the waterfront lots you could approximate the high-water line: it was still well downhill. Several miles in, the road reverted to caliche. Gordon's was just there, at the edge of development. The lot immediately uphill had stacked piles of steel I-beams and channels, getting ready for God knows. Gordon's lot was on the lake itself, and the driveway dropped quickly through some sizable cedar — you could make a beautiful tiny house there — and came out on an exposed hard limestone flat at the edge over the barren shore of the lake, clearly the spot for a House.

Gordon's minivan was parked under a large live oak at the far edge of the flat, blocking the view further west along the lake's edge. It was cool and windy even with the sun out. Gordon was sitting inside his van, but he got out and walked over as I pulled up. We started talking and my heart sort of instinctively fell. There just aren't a lot of interesting clients, and my first take on Gordon was that he belonged to that part of society for whom *Architecture* ranks below *Orthodontics.*

But I was nice enough. He began showing me photos of the house he'd seen, filed in a binder. These he described in excruciating detail, going so far as to comment on, for example, a bedspread that he didn't like, as if it might derail the design process. The house was just another graceless instant heritage limestone pile, over-proportioned, and too large too for the space there on the flat. What he saw in it — but I'd already decided it didn't matter: you could make some simple improvements. I was going to find some student to draft it, and we'd just pack it in. It seemed doable.

I interrupted his description of the photographs: "So, Gordon, what exactly is the *problem*?" The whole time we'd been standing in the middle of the flat, but now Gordon motioned me over to the north-facing lakeside edge, below and beyond which the gray limestone began that everywhere ringed the lake, with one startling exception, that had been invisible to me, as earlier it had been hidden from view behind Gordon's minivan and the oak.

The lot immediately to the west had been substantially *revisioned*. Where the high water line would normally, given the topography, have crossed quickly across that lot below the house, Gordon's neighbor's land instead bulged out into the lake in an immense lawn that eased down toward the water, while falling to either side, as if some gigantic, mossy sea turtle had pulled up to rest, burying its head beneath his neighbor's house. With the lake twenty feet down, the hump projected perhaps a hundred feet out, and it appeared to keep going under the water.

It was all man-made. Stepping along the property line down to the lake was a concrete retaining wall.

The surface of the hump was quilted with squares of St. Augustine grass that now, in early December, were tan and shriveled, seams showing where the grass had not taken. "In August when the lake was really down he just had one dump truck after another pour topsoil out there. It went on for days, the son of a bitch. We'd only closed on our lot for nine days. We tried all fall to back out of our contract, went to court, lost."

Yeah, I would have too: it was that ugly. Palm trees had been sporadically planted up near the house — of which all you could know was its mustard-yellow sprayed on stucco. Toward Gordon's side there was a palapa — it was unpainted treated lumber — with white Adirondack chairs underneath, and a hot tub and bar. At the tip of the hump there was a variable elevation floating dock with jet skis and two bug zappers. Strangest of all, anchored some hundred and fifty feet off the tip was an aluminum party barge with a hideous teal plastic roof. There was someone out on the barge — a woman — sitting in a deck chair reading. Maybe she had to get away to admire it all! Anyhow, I felt bad for Gordon. There was no way to excise any of it from your view of the lake, and, standing there, I knew it would be even more ugly one floor up.

But at least now I was interested. Nightmares like that — when the cycle of propriety is pretty well tossed out — sometimes lead to interesting work. So I just started talking: "You know, that *is* a problem. But maybe we could begin to think of the house not so much as a big box with windows, but perhaps as a series of stone fin walls that screen your view, like blinders on a horse. Or we could begin to imagine a house that capitalizes on a series of private gardens rather than the big view. After all, you know, after six months people with a single big view are usually sick of it ..."

I turned to see if any of this was registering with Gordon. He was looking at me slightly dumbfounded. Then suddenly he sharpened: "Oh, no — it's not going *here*! No, you're thinking — no, the house isn't going here!"

It was my turn to be stupid. "But where else can it go, up the hill in the cedar?"

"No, no" — he was grinning efficiently — "no, come on, let me show you. This is why I called."

Gordon started toward the water. The lake was about twenty feet down that day. I followed, stepping from one limestone ledge to the next below the flood line. There was a small army-green flat-bottomed boat tied up at the water's edge — actually it was attached to a form tie for the neighbor's retaining wall. I got in, and Gordon started the tiny electric fishing motor and pushed off, and as we slowly moved away from shore he began to explain: "All of the parcels along here run to the center of the lake. That's typically how land gets divided along a river, and Lake Travis is really the Colorado River. But if you look at where the center is" — he now pointed to the horizon — "well, that is a ways off to the west. The lots were platted with the water line in mind, but they still make it to the middle. So they have to angle west, and get thinner. Mine turns a couple of hundred feet out, under the water. It crosses in front of my neighbor right there where my wife is, out on our barge."

We had been heading out straight from shore, but as he spoke we turned toward the aluminum barge parked off the end of the hump. "We're still over my property here. I had it surveyed with divers. We chained the barge to three tethers on an expanding leash. If it's really windy out of the north, and the water is really low, then there's a statistical chance we might trespass." He was turning now to come alongside one of the aluminum pontoons, while his wife had gotten up as we approached. He turned to me and winked: "Son of a bitch would just have to come get me. Margie, here's the architect."

Gordon tied off the skiff. I shook hands with Margie. Her fingers were frozen from being out there in the wind. From the barge you could see farther up and down the lake, and it made the hump seem all the more perverse, even in that forsaken landscape. The whole house stared down at us through a huge glass picture window, like a Cyclops.

"So here," said Gordon, stamping on the deck, "here is where we are going to put the house. You just line it up with that picture window. It's about twenty feet down to stone today. You saw the steel coming in? I thought we could weld it first on shore and tow it out. We'll frame it just like an oil derrick. Fifty feet of welded steel cage — or I suppose we could bolt it up in pieces. The house just goes on top, a few feet above flood line. That steel is strong, and it should hold up my stone house. So here's my question: can you figure that cage out for me?"

It was heart breaking. Gordon paid me in cash, which he gave me in an unsealed envelope.

Keeping Austin Weird

Keeping Austin Weird

There are a series of barbeque joints positioned like Stations of the Cross in a ring of towns around Austin. One spring weekend I drove Axel and Sabina out to Llano, to eat at Cooper's. The rolling reddish ground everywhere was covered in a ridiculousness of bluebonnets, to the edge of the horizon, and the car floated along. In a valley filled with flowers we saw a lone emu, orphan of some failed agri-venture. A bit farther on we came upon a cowboy, fully duded out and saddled up, coming toward us through scrub cedar and cactus, riding herd on a flock of tiny Angora sheep, the legs of which disappeared into the purple blue.

Occasionally we passed cars parked on the side, the inhabitants out posing for pictures in the flowers. The Germans thought this was an idea, so we stopped, but Axel ended up standing on a fire ant mound. The stings — the pain takes a few seconds, just too long, to register, so that when you look down they are already swarming all over your shoes and legs — made him nauseous. Fire ants are a relatively recent wave of invaders, one of the suspected causes for the decline in horned lizards and quail. They have immense extended colonies with multiple queens, and no real enemies. To get rid of them you have to coordinate with your neighbors and poison every nest in as large an area as possible. Sabina took some photos of the welts with her phone.

After lunch we drove back by a long route, up through the Llano uplift toward Burnett, crossing Lake LBJ on the road there below the dam. The whole system of dams that control the Colorado as it passes from the hills to the prairie — Inks, LBJ, Mansfield, Tom Miller, Longhorn — is a particular sort of marvel. Lyndon Johnson cemented his political base in Texas as a young congressman by diverting substantial WPA funding (he had Roosevelt's ear) to get it all going, thereby electrifying the Hill Country, then the poorest region in the States. There used to be a bronze bust of LBJ at the state capitol, mounted in the marble niche of what had once been a water fountain. Busts should be mounted at correct anatomical height, because your mind unconsciously completes the figure. In that niche the bust sat, of course, too low. You felt LBJ sinking through the floor, to just the appropriate height for terrorizing children, or for reaching out and biting you somewhere inappropriate.

That was fixed when the capitol was recently renovated and expanded. The expansion was buried to the north of the existing building, to protect the views of it from around the city. Because the expansion is underground, cell phone reception there was initially really bad. You could look down into the circular exterior courtyard carved into the new building during breaks in the legislative sessions and see it filled with lobbyists and legislators on their phones. LBJ would have been at home in that pit. In Austin, you occasionally come across his name on old plat maps, penciled in as the owner: Lyndon Johnson et Ux. Ux — that would be Lady Bird. There are all of those stories about LBJ, and how he had perfected techniques for humiliating his subordinates into yet more excruciating loyalty. The story that sticks with me is about Johnson taking aides into the stall and making them stand there while he crapped, talking at them the whole time. I think of that story every time a client calls me on speakerphone. The sound is just like someone speaking from a toilet stall, while you're just being polite. Various people use speakerphone more than others. Not doctors, surprisingly, given the hygiene issues, but lawyers, in particular, in my experience.

I've had several lawyers as clients. Bill Norton was a lawyer when he hired me to design his house. It turned out I had seen him twice before I met him, once while looking into the cell phone pit at the capitol.

Bill was a notorious lobbyist, a fixture in the political world and the soft gossip columns of the newspapers, in a way that still just works in Texas, as a character. He was working then to persuade legislators to alter the definition of navigable rivers on behalf of property owners. In Texas, most rivers are legally navigable, meaning anyone has the right to move up or down them, as long as they don't set foot on the dry part of your land. Militant landowners point out the law made sense when it was in the public interest to move goods or settlers into territory, but it was not intended to protect an invasion of beer guzzling frat boys pontooning by. Bill stood out in the pit like a cartoon, in a suit and western boots, with one of those big silver beer-sopping mustaches, yelling into a tiny phone, and gesticulating broadly.

The mustache was what gave him away the second time I saw him, on that drive back from Llano. Crossing the dam at Lake LBJ on the four-lane highway, we came up behind a flock of motorcycles, mostly big new Harleys. When I was a kid that many motorcycles meant terror, but now every sunny weekend you come upon these coordinated middle-age fantasy outings, all collector hogs and designer leathers, going about five miles below the speed limit, everyone with headsets, moving like waves to or from worship at one of the barbeque stations.

"Is this a motorcycle gang?" Axel asked.

"Well, no, from the guts and the watches, I'd say this is most likely a law firm."

Axel looked perplexed.

Some fifty yards ahead of the pack was a lone Harley in the right lane. It was a beautiful bike, a yellow Sportster, nicely tricked out. The driver had on a black T-shirt, on the back of which, in orange letters, was written: *IF YOU CAN READ THIS THE BITCH FELL OFF*. So you had to look at the guy when you passed him, and there was the mustache. By coincidence, we first spoke several weeks later. Bill was finishing up divorce proceedings at the time. He was in an incredible hurry to get the house done. I asked him why he wanted to build instead of buy, and he made it clear that part of his reason was he wanted to piss off his ex. All along she had wanted to build something new. In the divorce she settled on his old house. He didn't have a lot of input, but it was clear from the start he wanted a house for the marketplace rather than too tight a fit to his own way of being. I know different people think differently about the relationship of house and home. I mean, for me, home connotes a sense of open-ended permanence, from which flows an ease about being consequent in the community. But I know people who change houses regularly — build one, sell it, build another. I know architects that do that — design a house, then abandon it. There was that sense with Bill, so there wasn't much point in pushing the matter.

Anyhow, he didn't have to worry either. The covenants on the lot were pretty severe. You had to design the house in a style that fit with the new old-age look of the community, with stone walls and multi-paned wood windows and overhanging pitched roofs, everything in earth tones, and there was an approved list of plants, and it was all controlled by a review committee. Really, it wasn't design in any conventional sense. It was more like remaking some recipe from a cookbook, only bigger, or just picking out items from a cafeteria line. To his credit, Bill kept the reins loose, with one exception. Whenever things started looking like an architect had done them — control, orderliness, abstraction, fetishism — he would realign the priorities. He was superbly pragmatic. He vetoed every good-looking built-in refrigerator for one that would fit a large pizza box.

The site was on the west side of Lake Austin, on the steep uphill side of that road running along the lake, in a gated cul-de-sac that squirmed along the contour like a large intestine: Water Oak Trail. The lot was toward the end, on the side closer to the lake. A dead end like that, running across a hill, is really two neighborhoods. The houses on the lower side look over the lake — they couldn't care less — and they casually turn their backs to the street. The more proper upslope houses forever have to peer over without seeming to. Usually they get really big windows, like dilated pupils.

What got me thinking about those windows was I had to spend time looking at them. This strange thing had happened. At the start of design Bill's site had been cleared of cedar in its upper reaches along the street, and, as his land bowed out slightly toward the lake, it opened terrific views up and down the valley. The lot was bookended by a stand of hackberries at the south end by the turnaround in the cul-de-sac, and a beautiful live oak at the north end, which was slightly downhill, a gorgeous tortured tree, not planted but native, fully sixty feet to the crown. After the cedar had been cleared, the hackberries and the live oak were the only things standing in the way of views up and down the river for several of the uphill sites, at least until the house was built. The hackberries were growing out of the stump of what had once been a substantial tree. Hackberries are nearly impossible to kill, and the trees there — now perhaps twenty feet tall — were sucker shoots, six trunks that started close together out of the cut stump of an older tree. Hackberries are extremely opportunistic, and with the clearing of the cedar this group had started filling out nicely.

A lot of people hate hackberries, as opposed to the vast cult of live oak lovers. A mature live oak can add tens of thousands of dollars of value to a piece of property. The city has a classification system for trees. There are all kinds of regulations if you want to cut down a live oak, but you can bring down a century-old hackberry and know the neighbors will approve. It's not just the warted skin. The limbs tend to develop small cracks in windstorms, which ice in when it freezes, then splinter. An old hackberry looks like King Lear, majestic and tragic. But who the hell wants King Lear around all the time? It would be like having to watch only Public Television. In the site plan the trees were fine, and they just stayed there, waiting to be thought about. I knew all along I wanted to replace them — I had mentioned it to Bill — but it was one of those perverse things, to ask your client to get rid of some trees, just to plant some trees in the same place, easier to accomplish when construction is well underway, when you can see it.

Live oaks though, well, it's hard to explain. There is an ancient oak in the city — the Treaty Oak. This man tried to poison it with a massive amount of herbicide in 1989, apparently to cast a spell. People *still* want him lynched. But, aside from idiots, oaks have their own problems, now. Foremost among these are the mysteries of oak wilt and oak decline. Oak decline is the general thinning of the oak canopy that seems to have occurred in recent years — acid rain? the dropping water table? global warming? Oak wilt is what happens when a particular beetle invades the body of the tree through a wound, a broken limb, a large cutting, over-zealous pruning. The beetles work their way into the tree's vascular system, slowly choking it. Entire areas of central Texas have been devastated by oak wilt — extraordinary trees, gone. Once oak wilt happens, there isn't a lot you can do. Tree doctors will come out and trench around the tree, to deny the spread through the roots, and pump poisons into the ground, halting the process. But the trees don't really recover. If you have healthy live oaks, you walk through your neighborhood scanning trees. Forget relaxing.

One morning as we were finishing the design drawings for neighborhood approval, I drove out to check some conditions at the site, and was startled to find the hackberries clearly and suddenly dead, their leaves brown and dry. I was actually somewhat relieved, because of wanting to get rid of those trees in the first place. Just as I was getting into my car I noticed there was also a substantial limb dead on the big live oak. *That* was cause for concern, because of oak wilt, and because, in the design of the house, the master bedroom opened onto a terrace under that tree. I called Bill, then called the city, which has a service to verify oak wilt.

They sent out an inspector the next day, a lean and wiry kid who looked like he'd just graduated from the Ag school at Texas A&M, very earnest and blank. While I was explaining the situation he kept looking at the dead stand of hackberries. I had to fill out some paperwork for him, and while I did so he strolled over to give the hackberries a look.

"I don't think oak wilt is your concern here," he said, coming back to the car.

"What do you mean?"

He looked straight at me. "Tell me again, you're not the owner, you're an architect?"

"Yeah, I'm here for the owner — but is there something wrong?"

"Well, we'll see," he said, grabbing climbing gear from his truck. He was walking over to the big oak when he turned and asked: "Have you filed your site development drawings yet?"

"No, not yet, why?"

"This oak is on your site plan?"

"The design of that end of the house sort of entirely depends on it."

He was quiet for a half a minute, thinking, then looked up into the oak, then back at me: "It looks like someone poisoned that hackberry. Whatever they used ran downhill and got this live oak."

"You're kidding!"

"See for yourself. Smells like someone poured gasoline on it." He started climbing.

I went over to the hackberries. All the grass around the stand was dead, in a perfect circle about five feet in diameter. I turned to look at the live oak across the lot: it was exactly downhill. A hotness came over me. For a minute I had the sense that I had done something wrong, or was to blame; then that lifted. I turned to look at the line of houses uphill around the cul-de-sac, three of them side-by-side, a little too close for their bulk, their huge fronts maxed out across their lots.

For all the sudden malevolence at work, there was only stillness, nothing moving on the lawns, or behind the various blank dark windows on either the first or second floors. That's when I first noticed how big those windows all were.

I walked over to that side of the street, and trespassed up onto one of the lawns. It had a hose bib in a flower garden that consisted of a steel sculpture of a dog, with one hind leg up, pissing running water into a watering can. Looking back toward the river, it was clear that each of the houses gained view up and down the river by the death of the hackberries, especially when you factored in the inevitability of Bill's new house blocking the water straight ahead. The inspector was now climbing down from the oak, so I walked back. "This tree is going to die. It doesn't look dead yet, but the core is dying. You might consider calling the police. I'll write you a report."

A policeman came out that afternoon. There was not much, it turned out, the police could do, short of asking all the neighbors if they'd seen anything. The officer implied this could be done in such a manner that would make it clear the police actually suspected whomever they were speaking to. I called Bill to talk about it, but he vetoed the idea. The house design had yet to be approved, so he didn't want to raise any resentment. As I said, he was superbly pragmatic. The whole thing was infuriating and it wasn't, like some distant political act. But the knowing I could not know — the hidden-in-plain-sight evil part — really bothered me. Who would do such a thing? I got the names of the various owners from the register of the homeowners association, and went online to try to get information about them. One was a third-generation chiropractor; another couple had worked for Dell. The third house was owned by two higher-ups in the University System office. I of course suspected the chiropractor, though there wasn't any actual evidence. There wasn't much to do but put it out of my mind.

I made arrangements to have the trees cut down. I knew this self-medicating longhair my cousin Kyle had gone to high school with, Duane Carlson. They were part of a big group that surfed together in Galveston in the late seventies, before Duane dropped out of school to slack in Austin. As the long-term viability of living day to day that way waned — one doctor's visit could destroy you financially — he had started a business, working out of his truck, that consisted primarily of removing ball moss from oak trees at expensive houses, and trying to sleep with any of the various women for whom he was working, apparently with some success.

I don't know how Duane pulled that last part off. He was another sort of anachronism you still meet here. Like a lot of guys I knew from Houston, he did not want to — or maybe just could not — take part in any sort of competitive economy, which he masked with a whole litany of conspiracy theories and impossibly idealistic socialisms. He had all kinds of theories about everything, and you could not get through an encounter with him without an almost endless cloud-lecture about how things should be. These were entertaining to a degree, and didn't necessarily have any hard relationship to how things actually were. If you scraped there wasn't really anything idealistic underneath either. Basically at the heart of it all was the unjustifiable hedonistic desire to, you know, sleep around, and life in Austin had always made sense because its sheen perfectly masked his constant horniness. Was there ever anything more attractive about hippydom for guys than the potential for justifiable commitment-free sex? I don't think so.

Anyway, it helped that Duane was good-looking, blond and blue-eyed, well defined, his body slightly hollow like other surfers, and pathologically positive. He had, over the years, hardened to wiry nut-brown muscled sinew, with abs like a teenager, even though he was in his fifties. The part I didn't get about his randy success was that he didn't make any conventional *effort* to be attractive. Because of his work, Duane was always covered with a fine sweat-glued layer of sawdust, and his long hair and beard were always sort of matted. He once told me he only showered in rainwater, but I never asked if he collected it, or just waited for storms to pass. Duane invariably made it clear that he never wore underwear — it was his starter conversation — beneath the same heavy pair of encrusted khaki work pants that he barely kept tied on with twine.

But, to his credit, his work was impeccable. He could move through a tree like fog, and would pluck the ball moss by hand off of each branch, no matter how small, as opposed to snipping the small branches off, or spraying the entire tree with baking soda, which are sloppier but less expensive ways to accomplish the same task. It took him days to clean a single tree, the better to get to know "… the lay of the land, and the land of the lay," as he put it. The thing with Duane was that you never knew *when* he was going to work — he would vanish for weeks — so on the day he actually got started I only found out because I had called to pester him about starting, and he told me he was already roped up in the tree and had several of the big limbs off the oak. On the phone he asked me if he could keep the wood for fires: "This stuff will light itself. You can still smell gasoline."

It was a hot, moist day. When I got to the site, Duane was taking a break, standing on the running board of the open cab of his severely beaten pickup, his shirt off, with a small square portable electric fan, rigged to the cigarette lighter on the dash, stuffed into the waistband of his pants, his twine belt dangling to his knees. He was talking with a woman in jogging gear — one of the neighbors it turned out — about removing ball moss at her house. Duane was giving her his smiling lecture about the wrong-headed conspiracy-ness of every conventional form of arboreal treatment. He was completely focused on the woman, and his whole body language was forward and confident — at one point he raised his left arm from the top of the open truck door and plucked some dirt from his armpit mid-sentence — even with his pants legs alternately billowing out as he shifted his stance. He didn't look at me until his conversation with her was done, and only then after he had watched her walk all the way back to her own front door. He didn't make any attempt to hide his leering desire, and everything about it was just so pleasantly wrong.

It turned out that, in a morning's work, he had managed to get jobs at several of the houses on the street — he wasn't cheap, but there he was — and, one eyebrow lifted, he noted the "potential" of the block. After he'd cleared Bill's trees, I occasionally saw his truck parked up and down the street for the next several months — it stood out against the grain of that neighborhood, as he put it, "Like a preacher's dick in a nudist colony." And then he vanished again.

A year and a half passed. The design was easily approved and the house was built — it was nothing you could even photograph without shame — and Bill moved in, and we planted new trees, and the whole sad strangeness of the dead trees evaporated from my mind.

About six months after the house was finished I was waiting in the drive-through of a roast chicken stand east of the interstate, when Duane's truck pulled up behind me in line. I got out and walked back to say hello, and he said he had a good story to tell me about Bill's dead tree — from his wink I instantly knew there was some post-coital component — so we got our food and parked, and ate at a picnic table they had there set out in the parking lot.

"It *was* the chiropractor."

"What?! I *knew* it — I *knew* it! How'd you figure it out? Did the wife tell you? You slept with the wife, didn't you? I can't *believe* you slept with the wife!"

"Patience, my young friend, patience."

He pulled meat off a chicken thigh and wrapped it in a tortilla.

"Now David you may remember the wife — Alex — did you ever see her? Gorgeous and put together, with a tennis ass and real tits, just distracting. I was after her for weeks. I would time my breaks to meet her coming in and out, and we would talk a bit, and she would bring me something to drink wearing, like, a T-shirt, and it was clear she was *thinking* about it. I'd be up in the trees, and she would open the blinds in whatever room she was in. She wouldn't exactly look at me, but she wouldn't hide either. It just drove me nuts. Then the husband would come home in the late afternoon and they would come out and she would be all cool and demanding about the work, but whenever he would turn away she would, like, warm up.

"Well, they had this one tree with an impossible limb that hung out over their swimming pool in back of the house — it was about twenty feet up. I'd been avoiding going out on it because of all the leaf litter that would end up in the pool, plus it was a real bitch because it was tough to rope off — it was all balance.

"So finally one day I go out on that limb, and there I am out there concentrating like a game show contestant, when out of the corner of my eye I see Alex walk out of the house and get in the pool — but, as I said, I am focused on the *tree*. So she's floating around the pool on this inflatable raft, and the breeze is moving her back and forth, but I'm not getting any kind of good look because the wind is bouncing the limb up and down. It isn't until she floats right underneath my limb that I realize she has nothing on. I mean, nothing — NOTHING! — Not. A. Thing. She's laying on her back on that float, with her arms under her head, and just as she passes underneath me, she ... well, she sorta *spreads* her legs a little bit, and smiles up at me at the same time."

"You are such a liar!"

"God's own truth, my friend: she's smiling, *it's* smiling ..."

He rolled up another tortilla.

"So there I am standing on that stupid limb, and I'm staring down at her as she floats past, and — OK, this never happens to me — I lose my fucking balance. It's entirely possible my hard-on relocated my center of gravity. I grab air and tumble straight out of the tree into the pool — thank God there's a fucking pool!"

"So at least you hit the water."

"Smacked it like roadkill!"

"But what about your harness — didn't it stop you before you hit?"

"Well ..." Duane paused to take a bite, and looked at me out of the corner of his eye, "I did manage to unhook that before I got too dizzy."

"God, you are such a dog!"

"And let me tell you Dave, it was a dog's day in that pool: a little fetch, a little roll over, a little doggy paddle ... *ARF, ARF!*"

"Look," I held up my hand, laughing, "I don't even want to know about your, about this ... *Lady and Tramp* scenario. Just tell me how she told you about the tree."

"Well, *she* didn't tell me."

"But then how did you find out it was her husband?"

"Oh, he told me."

"*He* told you?"

"Sort of. I'm getting to that."

He poured more hot sauce onto his half-eaten tortilla.

"So, the thing is, I cut them a good deal on the work. Dude, it was worth it. I arranged a service contract — show up every two weeks, prune a bit, and then, uh, you know, trim the shrubbery. I would do a couple of days of work, and then we'd find some way to get it on. Like, one time she takes me to this couch they have made of cow horns — like actual longhorn long horns — and I'm on my back grabbing on to these horns —"

"Duane. Please."

"Right." Duane sighed. "So, anyway, last week I'm out there late one afternoon, up in this tree, and he comes out of the house and starts yelling at me to come down immediately — clearly he's pissed off.

"So I climb down and he starts getting all in my face, yelling at me about *assaulting his wife*. I'm like, 'what in the hell are you talking about,' and he starts waving around this DVD and these printouts. He launches in about how he's been backing up the security camera files from the house and he's come across frames of me falling — *jumping* he says — out of that tree."

"Oh, shit!"

"NO shit! In my head I'm thinking I'm completely fucked. I have no excuse lined up. But, it also becomes clear to me that he doesn't have the whole story. He's going on about me *trying to rape his wife*. The pictures he's got are only exposures every half a minute or so, and it doesn't cover the whole pool. All he's got are pictures of me jumping — I mean *falling* — out of the tree and what looks like me chasing after his wife in the pool. The pictures are really grainy — you can't tell very much — but there is definitely *something* not right. And so I'm guessing Alex has told him some bullshit story, because he's going on and on about this 'attack.'

"Of course, I deny the whole thing. But it's hard to do convincingly — I mean, the pictures are clear enough. The only defense I can think of is: *why would I still be working here if I had tried to attack your wife*? But I don't say that. I know the thought must have crossed his mind too — it has to have! — and it's clear he doesn't quite believe her either, and that he's after me to tell him what he already suspects."

"He must have known …"

"Yeah, actually, I knew he probably knew. I mean, how stupid do you have to be? He wasn't really listening to anything I said anyway, even though I was staying really calm. He kept getting more and more aggressive, and yelling louder and louder at me, and poking me in the chest, and going on about calling the police, and finally he gets so worked up — I thought his face was going to explode — that he pulls out his phone and starts dialing."

"The police?"

"Yeah, the police. He said: 'I am CALLING the police.' I'm like, *FUCK*! I am *not* seeing any way out of this. So, in desperation, I grab for the only thing I've even remotely got left. I just yell at him — at the top of my lungs — '*HEY*! If you're calling the cops, turn your fucking *self* in! You fucking poisoned that tree, you *fucking TREE POISONER!*'

"I mean, I didn't know, but it was all I had. And, David, let me tell you: it was a stroke of pure *Grade A fucking luck*. The guy just freezes up, and you can see him start doing the math in his head. And then he knew what was going down, because he storms up to the house and throws open the door and yells: '*You TOLD him? You FUCKED him and then TOLD him?*'

"Well, my friend, that was all the opening I needed to get the hell out of there. Left my ropes, left my gear ..."

Later I told the story to Axel and Sabina. Sabina said that the word for poison in German is *Gift*. Axel thought about it for a few moments. "It is a nice story, but I do not think it can possibly be true."

"How do you figure?"

"Really, David? I mean, it is ridiculous, don't you agree? And the coincidences are impossibly perfect. The whole thing seems — to me — to be some sort of improbable tree pornography."

"But, Axel, why should he tell me a lie?"

Axel shrugged his shoulders, "Perhaps he is just helping to keep Austin weird."

Gatherings on the Line

Gatherings on the Line

If you look at a geological map of Texas, the right half is dirt — essentially the mudflats of the great ancient inland sea — and the left half is rock — essentially the toe of the uplift that crests in the Rockies. Austin sits right on the line between. You have to think that early settlers, inexorably pushing west across endless miles of fertile soil, must have looked up at that edge of rock in dismay: "Damn it. We've gone too far." That said, there are advantages to an edge in the middle. Either side of the line defines a way to be — dirt farmer, cattle rancher. But the border is always something else, not the product of both.

One consequence of Austin's specific topography is that there are many advantageous places to live. It isn't like Dallas or Houston or San Antonio, where in each there is a pyramid of desirability at the apex of which there are at best two or three neighborhoods that are really wanted — despite the millions of people, the millions of lots. The hills above the springs, or west of the lake, the ridge along Shoal Creek, the various high ground along the lakes, or south of the river looking to the capitol, the older neighborhoods north and east of the University of Texas — the list goes on, and no one part of the city claims precedence. You meet people happily settled everywhere, and the map of consequent dwelling is like the pattern of the night sky.

There are places no one builds houses though — the dark nothing in between bands of stars — where various washes that drain the high ground cut deeply into the fabric of the city. These small valleys form the vast part of the informal public space of Austin, the public space construed by common private experience instead of ceremony. In them you often find old public swimming pools — a rectangle of water, a concrete deck, a stone bathhouse, a fence, trees beyond in the middle ground. All of these pools redefine the public realm on warm late afternoons, as work stops and a more fundamental order reasserts itself.

For a while I regularly swam at Deep Eddy, the largest and oldest of these floodplain pools. Deep Eddy exists in an inexplicable loophole in the city. The jogging trail around Town Lake doesn't seem to reach it. When the trail loops back under the MoPac bridge, the whole riverbank towards Deep Eddy seems ignored. The little appendix of trail leading from the runners' stretching area under the bridge to the pool vanishes into those woods quickly and uncertainly, densely lined with poison ivy, mustang grape, and trash trees. And the street at the end of which Deep Eddy lurks, when you pass it on Lake Austin Boulevard just west of the MoPac, looks like a service driveway. When you do finally find it — having heard of it frequently enough, but in the end someone almost has to show you where it is — it still doesn't seem to be there. You pull onto the big flat parking lot sitting on the bluff of the 100-year floodplain that drops away so swiftly you think the river is just below. Along the far edge of the asphalt there is a fence set amid pecan trees, harbingers of water and flooding. There is the mute stone wall of the bathhouse on the left, but it just continues the tangle of the forest.

The only clues were once a great stand of cottonwoods beyond the pecans. When you finally came to the edge, and looked down on the glorious geometry of the pools — two uncompromised, connected, blue rectangles, the big one on the right getting deeper from ankle to abdomen, and the lap pool on the left with its deep lanes running toward the river — the flickering of the cottonwood leaves in the sun mirrored the shimmering of the water's surface, forming a half-domed amphitheater. That sense was sharpened by the opaque brush along the river and the lawn beyond the lap lanes, and by the sloping grassed grade dropping down from the parking lot and the west. Recently all of those Cottonwoods were found to be diseased, and they were cut down, but the newly planted trees are hopeful. You enter under an awning where you pay, then a concrete stairway drops you to the edge of the pool, passing through the site like a catheter, and the city is gone, in a reciprocal agreement about disappearance. To sit you step back up onto a bench-high stone wall that retains the narrow grass field that surrounds the pools.

It is hard to imagine any American city producing a public space so austere and rich today. But, in truth, the pool was a private amusement park before it was sold to Austin: it had, for example, a diving tower for horses. Deep Eddy — the name — is a memory of a dangerous current in the Colorado formed by an immense underwater boulder that was dynamited for safety. The clear cold water is pumped over from the aquifer at Barton Springs across the river.

In the morning, the shadows of the surrounding trees blanket the lap lanes, which you have to yourself. In the afternoon, the sun burns that end of the pool, heating the low stone walls and the concrete deck, as you sit there steeling yourself against the shock of getting in. During the mid-afternoon, swimmers tend to divide the lanes in half, extending a politeness that begins with an informal system of recognizing who is next, without there having to be any sort of waiting line. Then, sometime in the late afternoon, it gets crowded, and the lanes triple up and start looping. With luck the swimmers in any one lane are of roughly the same ability, but occasionally some swim-Nazi will jump in, churning the water like a powerboat. Or sometimes someone will clog a lane for walking aerobics. It's better to wait until early evening, when the vapor lamps go on, like swimming in bright moonlight.

On Saturday nights in the summer you can sometimes watch movies there while floating in the cold water: they set up a projection screen on the long river side of the shallower pool. All kinds of people come, not just families with kids. Sabina and Axel had gotten into going, and they pestered me about it often enough that I finally went with them, to see Creature from the Black Lagoon in old-style 3-D. Actually, the scene was pretty great. There were perhaps a hundred and fifty people on various kinds of floats, all wearing paper and gel film glasses, filling the pool in clusters. Someone was trying to get the whole group to start a standing wave. The sunlight was almost gone, and two screech owls began making their weird quavering wails from the trees along the river.

Axel and Sabina had floats. I ended up sitting on the edge of the pool directly opposite the screen, just next to a lifeguard stand, my legs dangling in the water. It was a great place to sit in the dark. The mirrored image of the creature staggering out of the water rippled and reflected across the entire surface of the pool between the various people. Perhaps fifteen feet in front of me was a couple with three kids. The parents were lying on their chests across an air mattress with their young daughter sitting between them, their two older sons — perhaps six and nine — moving around them in swim rings. The boys had lost interest in the film and had drifted behind their parents. They were trying to outdo each other, making creature gills with their hands. I watched them for a while, then turned back to the movie. When I looked again, the younger one was gone. I sat there stupid for what must have been five seconds, when suddenly the water right in front of me exploded: it was the lifeguard who had jumped over my head from the stand, halfway to the empty ring. Just as she went down to grab the kid, another lifeguard hurled past me into the water.

They got the kid out of the pool sputtering and gasping, and sat him on the low wall just behind where I had been — everyone cleared back. The kid's vitals checked out: he was just scared out of his wits. The film had been stopped and the vapor lamps were slowly coming on in fits and starts. Everyone was staring at the lifeguards working. From where I was it was a strange sight, looking out: all of these wet people in the flickering light with their red-and-green glasses, craning for a better look, which caused the various floats to bob up and down madly. The lifeguards had nonetheless managed to make a calm eye in the middle of this storm. I turned to a woman who was standing next to me with her two girls and mentioned that I was impressed by how capable but relaxed the lifeguards were being. She said: "I think they're just getting him to relax, so that when they talk to him more seriously, which they will do in a bit, he'll hear it."

One of the two girls looked up and said: "When Mom wants us to do something she tells the life-guards to tell us."

I met Claire and Reed Michaels at Deep Eddy. We would arrive at the same time, and started talking while waiting for lanes. They had just moved to Austin from Palo Alto, to teach at UT — they were both historians. They had a chunk of cash from selling their house near Stanford, enough to build something decent. For me, they were the first clients who actually got architecture. Maybe it had to do with life in

California, or that they were academics, but they were just really open to the possibilities of how a house might liberate them. They both wrote a lot, and were concerned to have changing places to write — actually to think in clearly. They didn't have children, which comes with its own set of advantages. What they wanted was a series of frames of reference, rooms that were not committed to a particular function, but could be used according to their advantage, a sort of matrix of options and vulnerabilities. It may sound unusual to describe the house that way, but we were sitting around half-naked, without paper and pencil, when we were talking about it, so the house had to be construed in words first.

They had already bought a lot in a part of Austin called Hyde Park, just north of the university. Hyde Park was the city's first suburban expansion — the first moonlight tower was installed there. Most of the houses are Arts and Crafts bungalows, starter houses now, but dream homes in the late 19th century, on small lots with alleys. It was all built at a time when there was perhaps a greater collective sense of propriety. During the sixties and seventies its families died out, or moved to larger lots slightly farther out, and Hyde Park gradually became the haunt of college students and young graduates and professors. It has a lovely anarchic sleepy seedy charm, set under its now fully grown trees.

The charm isn't just physical. You can get some sense of that just before Christmas on the blocks of 37th Street just east of Guadalupe. The inhabitants along the street put up their decorations as a conspiracy. Strings of lights begin at one house, yet pass easily over the gathered neighbors to another and another, past the milling pedestrians laughing at the house covered with lights still in their plastic packaging frames nailed like wallpaper to every inch of exposed siding, at the crèche composed solely of Ratfinks, at the Volkswagen van entirely filled with a diorama of Troll cult Christmas scenes. Lights are strung over the street, on lamps and fire hydrants and stop signs, so that property and infrastructure and privacy are pleasantly blurred. Even though it has tamed down, real effort still goes into making it seem that no standards are being upheld, whatsoever. Supposedly architecture students living in one of the houses started the whole thing. It's possible. They would have had to be students to see something that clearly. For me, a lot of Austin is bound up in the possibilities that vision affords. I talked about it a lot with Claire and Reed, because of the resonance to what they had described at Deep Eddy.

But, really, Hyde Park, it's a hard place to build. All of it is vulnerable, like all such places, vulnerable and fragile. On the one hand, that way of small living now offers its appeal against the gated overlarge nowhere-ness of the outlying suburbs. On the other, Hyde Park is prime real estate, close in to the center, ready and ripe to be remembered with a vengeance by the new house, the new privacy, the new not neighborliness. Hyde Park residents have worked with the city to enact a kind of zoning protection to preserve the feel of the neighborhood. It isn't as severe as a historic district — where you have to build in the style of — but when you apply for a building permit there is a separate review to ensure that the character of the neighborhood will not be destroyed. The city had organized a series of design guidelines to try to get architects to make new houses look just like the old ones. The guidelines are not strictly enforceable, but the neighborhood has a supremely organized, self-policing component in its organization and in the watchful communication of its constituents.

That kind of compliance, I just have an allergic reaction to the idea. Part of it has to do with the impossibility of making something new like something old. It is not the look part — not the difficulty of drawing an old cottage or getting labor to do the same level of detail. It is the dwelling in a replicant part, the feel part. It's like wearing a fake Rolex watch, or men who live with wives or girlfriends with breast implants. It isn't that you can't fool everyone else, it's that you know yourself, and so doubt creeps into the relationship. And then there is the whole death of hope about how the future might be. I understand where it comes from, but the compliance somehow directly contradicts half of the thing being protected.

Anyhow, the house was going to be small — smaller than what the zoning allowed — and we could make an argument about character, so Claire and Reed agreed to let the neighborhood-look thing go in favor of open design exploration, though they asked me to make a big model with the neighboring houses in it, as a sort of check. The design developed into a line of repetitive, austere flat-topped stone boxes, pushed along the long north edge of the lot, that were bound together by a minimal porch running east-west the full depth of the site. Each of the boxes opened through big wood-framed windows to a different orientation: one to the sky and a corner of the moonlight tower in the distance, one to a low vegetable garden, one to the top of a large gum tree in the neighboring backyard, one fully to the street. Between the boxes were the functional components: bathrooms, an outdoor shower, closets, the kitchen, fireplaces.

To move from box to box, you went out onto the porch, part of which was screened. There were no steps up into the house, and all of the paving passed inside to out. The edge of the porch was a gutter at grade filled with gravel that collected all the rainwater off the boxes. In a big storm, the porch was another room, with one edge a wall of water. All of the rooms opened to the porch with large rolling shuttered doors, and, depending on the exposure of each to the sun, had differing kinds of shades or curtains, to screen from none to absolute. To enrich the various privacies, a stone wall wove through the boxes and formed small spaces adjacent to the rooms.

With the overlarge simple windows and the stone garden wall and the repetitive stone boxes, it ended up looking pretty abstract. But it was optimistic, and largely hidden by a big garden that also ran the whole length of the lot, and Claire and Reed were really happy with it: they could see how their lives were going to work. But they were also worried about offending the neighbors — the neighborhood being part of their desire to live there. They decided that the best thing to do was to show them what we were going to build. I thought it was a bad idea — better to get the architecture done and pick up the pieces, rather than have it killed by good intentions. We actually ended up arguing about it, but Reed and Claire insisted. They scheduled it for a Saturday afternoon. As a fair trade, or an olive branch, Claire offered me her ticket to the football game at the university afterward.

They arranged a get-together at the house of one their lot's immediate neighbors. Five couples were going to be there: the people on both sides, and all of the people from the three houses across the way. Everyone was already there when we walked up to the house. Up on the front porch there was a wooden swing seat, and four recycling bins, and fifteen or twenty pairs of shoes left lying around. Fixed to the transom window over the door was a bumper sticker: Handgun-free Zone. It was a nice group of people inside, of varying ages, everyone casual in shorts or cotton dresses, mostly barefoot, which explained all the shoes on the porch. There wasn't a lot of makeup, or energy wasted on hair, or apparent plastic surgery. Almost everyone looked fit: it was like something out of a new-age clothing catalogue. Claire and Reed were concerned to make friends, and vice versa. So for a while there was nothing for me to do but hang back out of the conversation, which kept tacking away from the house design, and to past lives and things in common. Everyone was busy inspecting Claire and Reed as if they were newly landed exchange students — or, if not doing that, they were surreptitiously studying the model.

To avoid premature questions, I ended up poking around the house. The whole thing consisted of two small one-story wood-sided rectangular buildings — each essentially a house — set at right angles to each other. I asked Karen, one of the owners, about it. She said: "This house was built by a woman who was having a long-running secret affair with the married man who lived in the lot just behind us. Her mother also lived with her, so to keep that arrangement working she built two houses."

A kid came in and spoke to Karen in Spanish:

"[Travis won't let me use the computer.]"

"[Please ask him to turn it off for now and read.]"

"[But Mom, it's my turn.]"

"[Sweetheart: reading!]"

I asked: "Do you only speak Spanish at home?"

"Actually we normally speak German. But we have a live-in student from the university who speaks only Spanish with the kids."

As we were talking, the meeting was coming to order. Reed had set the model onto a low table that had been moved to the center of a ring of chairs and couches. He was explaining the overall orientation — where each person lived relative to the model. He then asked me to describe the why of the house. I started talking about living in Austin, and how much Hyde Park held out hope for a way of life, but I may have rambled a bit, because one of the neighbors asked: "David, I apologize for jumping in, but is that part where there is nothing, is that meant to be glass?" He had moved off his chair and was crouching down, looking at the front of the house.

"It is. We'd like for the house to be really open, you know, to the trees, and the neighborhood, and the sky, and ..."

"So, is it missing the window frames?"

"No, that's how it would be, with large sheets of glass."

"Can you do that? I mean, can the glass hold itself up?"

"Sure, not a problem." I didn't want to lose the gist of the ideas, but before I could get back on track, another neighbor interjected: "And the roofs are all flat?"

"They are. Each of the rooms of the house is like a box."

I explained the idea of the different uses of the rooms, and their different orientations and realities — "to keep the experience complete, the ceiling on the inside and the roof on the outside match each other."

"Won't there be a problem with leaking, with a flat roof?"

"There shouldn't be. You can make a really good flat roof now, that will last for thirty years."

"Wouldn't it be the same experience," someone else asked, "if they were pitched? I mean, do you or can you see the roof from inside?"

"Well, you know that's an interesting philosophical question. I don't think it is the same. When you know the roof is flat, then the ceiling has a more immediate relationship with the sky ..."

One of the neighbors said, calmly: "I have a pitched metal roof. When it rains I hear the sky."

"David, can I ask another question about the glass in front: would there be, like, curtains or something?"

"Oh, sure ..." I tried to start in again about vulnerability —

"What if you pitched the roofs and sloped the ceilings inside?" I turned to get to that question, but the person who had asked it was already speaking with her couch-mate, and they were using their hands to reimagine the planes of the ceilings.

"Why is the porch on the side?"

"Well, that side faces south, so the porch acts to shade the rooms from the summer sun."

"Could it wrap around the front?" Someone passed over a pad of paper for the questioner to make a sketch — "How do you mean?" The conversation, running along on its own, was now largely out of control. Claire and Reed had been pulled into separate discussions. I could see them nodding earnestly. I heard Claire say, "Of course we could consider that…"

One of the neighbors turned to me: "I saw a house sort of like this in Santa Fe. It was an old adobe building with six square rooms in a grid. All the rooms were the same. Each wall either had a door or a window in the middle. The two rooms in the center had been opened up into one large room — but the other four rooms were identical. Only one was now a bathroom, one was a kitchen, and the other two were bedrooms. It was really a strange old house. It didn't matter where things went. I should send you some pictures of it."

"Actually, David, all of these garden walls look like they belong in Santa Fe …"

"What are those walls made of?"

"Limestone …"

"I don't know that I have seen many stone walls in the neighborhood."

It went on in that swarming, bouncing way for another half an hour. Here's the thing: it wasn't awful. People were asking questions and making comments politely, without seeming to judge. They weren't outwardly negative or positive. But it also didn't really matter what I said. I guess that's fine, but I was really worried it would affect Claire and Reed.

Finally, someone asked: "David, how far along is the design at this point?" Suddenly the room quieted down.

"I would like to say that we are really close to being finished."

It stayed quiet for some seconds.

Reed spoke up: "We still have some ways to go."

After we left, Claire and Reed were distracted. As I was putting the model in the car I asked Claire what she thought. "Reed and I are going to have to talk about it. Then we can get together in a couple of days." The afternoon was almost gone, and it was time to head over to the university for football. Reed and I decided to walk. It was hot and clear passing south through Hyde Park and across the ever-denser campus to the packed stadium. Reed didn't talk a whole lot, and especially not about the house.

It was a long, hot climb up to the seats, which were near the top of the old upper deck. But up there at least a breeze was moving, and you could see the capitol and downtown to the south, and the vast sea of burnt-orange shirts of the UT fans below, a huge noisy swarm confined in the almost closed oval of the stadium. We were sitting behind a row of really large white guys in burnt-orange collared sports shirts — young alumni — all wearing their UT caps backward. I guess that made sense: the late sun was to our backs.

The Longhorns — the UT team — got off fast, scoring 24 points in the first quarter, and holding their opponents, the TCU Horned Frogs, to nothing. It was the beginning of a rout. Every time the Longhorns scored, a group of students in cowboy attire on the field set off a cannon. At the start of the second quarter, TCU had the ball on its own 3-yard line, and tried a forward pass to the 20. But the Longhorn defensive back clearly hit the TCU receiver too soon, and the referee's yellow flag was up before the play even ended, the ball bouncing erratically down the field. The stadium erupted in mad hooting and hoarse aggressive catcalling at the officials. The guys in front of us were on their feet in a pressing line, cursing and yelling. You know, I hate football. At the half the Longhorns were up something like 45 to 3.

During the half time break the TCU band played first — loose, strutting, oiled — but the performance didn't get much of a rise from the people in the stands. Then the UT band moved out onto the field like a weather front. The band started tightly compressed in one entire end zone, from which it slowly and evenly expanded, like the bellows of a spreading accordion, fully over the length and width of the field, from one end zone to the other, in a beautiful widening diamond crosshatch geometry, with the last row stationary on the starting end line. When the front row found the opposite end line, the whole band stopped, and slowly and perfectly collapsed back in on itself again, every row of band members moving at a slightly different rate from all the others, to finally compress back to its origin all at the same moment. The whole expansion and contraction — the breathing of the huge band — was perfectly timed to the length of UT's striding victory march. It was mind-achingly simple and powerful, and a swelling roar filled the stadium.

Then the band did something more perfect still. One person at a time, it uncoiled from the end zone in a single unctuous line, that, squirming over the field as one member followed the next, slowly spelled out the word Texas, one letter after another, connected in a continuous looping script, as if it had been properly written there by the invisible prim hand of some elderly librarian. It was like watching as the pen actually formed the word, in a kind of flowing lilting handwriting that you don't see anymore. Script Texas.

For some reason — the day, the house, the heat, the orange crowd, the green of the field, and the city on the horizon — I was overcome with a rising sad tightness. I don't know. In front of me one of the big guys, talking to his neighbor, reached under his shirt, and you could see, from the angle of his arm, and the way the burnt orange fabric bunched up, that he was probably reaching for a pimple on his back. Reed turned to me suddenly and said: "I don't think it is going to be worth the trouble." We talked a bit, mostly about holding off on a decision like that. The slaughter continued on the field, and midway through the third quarter Reed excused himself. I was about to follow him, but decided instead to climb to the top of the stands, to see out to the west, over the hills. But there was not much there, as the stadium wall was designed so you couldn't see over the top, beyond the glow of the sky at sunset.

Though I am an architect in Austin — and I did design a house for someone who insisted on a refrigerator deep enough for a pizza box — this book is entirely a work of fiction. To my beloved clients: rest assured, you do not appear in these stories.

Parts of this book were completed at the American Academy in Rome, the Museum of Fine Arts Houston Dora Maar House, The Rockefeller Foundation Bellagio Center, and the Bogliasco Foundation Liguria Study Center. I'm grateful to Nancy Levinson and Josh Wallaert for graciously publishing two of the stories at Places Journal. Thank you Rick Pappas for time tending to the legalities. I am honored to be working with Dino Price, and the John M. Hardy Press.

This book certainly would not have happened if my wife Sandy and I had not visited our friend John Stokes in Austin many years ago. And some of the stories would have been difficult to imagine without the adventures of our daughter Helen, her particular friends, and their extended families. Finally, our son Walter line edited this manuscript with remarkable insight and precision: thank you.